She was kissing her boss.

More than that, she was making out like a crazed teenager with the very man judging her professionalism.

Maybe this was a test. It was probably a test. She'd passed weapons proficiency only to fail miserably at self-control. Mila scrambled to salvage the situation, seizing on the first idea she had. "What about me going to South America with the team?"

"Are you kidding me?"

She brazened it out, walking her fingertips up his chest. "I speak pretty good Spanish."

Troy trapped her hand with his, squeezing it tight. "You're telling me that kiss was just about persuasion?"

She looked him straight in the eye. "Of course it was persuasion."

"You're lying."

* * *

The Baby Contract
is part of Harlequin Desire's #1 bestselling series
Billionaires and Babies: Powerful men...
wrapped around their babies' little fingers.

Dear Reader,

After writing more than forty books for Harlequin, I find myself thinking about new approaches to the romances I've loved to write.

I've always enjoyed creating contemporary stories with a classic romantic foundation. *The Baby Contract* is a contemporary story, but with a bit of a suspenseful twist.

Troy Keiser is the formidable owner of Pinion Security Company. It's the best in the country and the only place rookie agent Mila Stern wants to work. Troy doesn't hire women. But when his little sister Kassidy, a budding pop singer, shows up with an adopted baby looking for Troy's protection, he agrees to let Mila help out.

What starts as a quasi-babysitting assignment soon turns into a truly dangerous situation, revealing shocking secrets and forcing Troy and Mila to depend on each other to protect Kassidy and the baby.

Thanks for coming along on the adventure. I do hope you enjoy the story!

Barbara

THE BABY CONTRACT

BARBARA DUNLOP

Recycling programs
for this product may
not exist in your area.

ISBN-13: 978-0-373-73409-2

The Baby Contract

Copyright © 2015 by Barbara Dunlop

Printed in U.S.A.

www.Harlequin.com

Barbara Dunlop writes romantic stories while curled up in a log cabin in Canada's far north, where bears outnumber people and it snows six months of the year. Fortunately she has a brawny husband and two teenage children to haul firewood and clear the driveway while she sips cocoa and muses about her upcoming chapters. Barbara loves to hear from readers. You can contact her through her website, barbaradunlop.com.

Books by Barbara Dunlop

Harlequin Desire

An After-Hours Affair
A Golden Betrayal
A Conflict of Interest
The Missing Heir
The Baby Contract

Colorado Cattle Barons

A Cowboy Comes Home
A Cowboy in Manhattan
An Intimate Bargain
Millionaire in a Stetson
A Cowboy's Temptation
The Last Cowboy Standing

Chicago Sons

Sex, Lies and the CEO
Seduced by the CEO

Visit the Author Profile page at Harlequin.com or barbaradunlop.com for more titles.

For my daughter

One

Troy Keiser halted his razor midstroke, glancing to the phone on the bathroom counter.

"Say again?" he asked his business partner, Hugh "Vegas" Fielding, sure he must have misheard.

"Your sister," Vegas repeated.

Troy digested the statement, bringing the cell to his ear, avoiding the remnants of his shaving cream. Sandalwood-scented steam hung in the air, blurring the edges of the mirror.

"Kassidy is *here*?"

His nineteen-year-old half sister, Kassidy Keiser, lived two hundred miles from DC, in Jersey City. She was a free spirit, a struggling nightclub singer, and it had been more than a year since Troy had seen her.

"She's standing in reception," said Vegas. "Seems a little twitchy."

Last time Troy had seen Kassidy in person, he was in Greenwich Village. A security job with the UN had brought him to New York City, and the meeting was purely by chance. Kassidy had been playing at a small club, and the diplomat he'd been protecting wanted an after-hours drink.

Now, he glanced at his watch, noting it was seven forty-five and mentally calculating the drive time to his morning meeting at the Bulgarian embassy. He hoped her problem was straightforward. He needed to solve it and get on with his day.

"You'd better send her up."

He dried his face, put his razor and shaving cream in the cabinet, rinsed the sink, and pulled a white T-shirt over his freshly washed hair, topping a pair of black cargo pants. Then he went directly to the kitchen and poured himself a cup of coffee, downing it to bring his brain cells back to life.

His and Vegas's side-by-side apartments took up the top floor of the Pinion Security Company building in northeast

DC. The first two floors housed the company's reception and meeting areas. Floors three to seven were offices and electronic equipment storage. The computer control center was highly secured, directly below the apartments. The basement and subbasement were used for parking, target practice and storage for a vault of weapons.

The building was state-of-the-art, built after Troy sold his interest in some innovative security software and Vegas hit it big at a casino on the strip. After that, their company had grown exponentially, and they'd never looked back.

The buzzer sounded, and he crossed the living room, opening the apartment door to find the six-feet-four, barrel-chested Vegas standing behind his sister, Kassidy, who, even in four-inch heels, seemed barely half the man's size. Her blond hair was streaked purple, and she wore three earrings in each ear. A colorful tunic-style top flowed to a ragged hem at midthigh over a pair of skintight black pants.

"Hello, Kassidy." Troy kept his voice neutral, waiting to ascertain her mood. He couldn't imagine it was good news that brought her here.

"Hi, Troy." She slanted a gaze at Vegas, clearly hinting that he should leave.

"I'll be downstairs," said Vegas.

Troy gave his partner a short nod of appreciation.

"Is everything okay?" he asked as Kassidy breezed her way into the penthouse foyer.

"Not exactly," she said, hiking up her oversize shoulder bag. "I have a problem. At least I think it's a problem. I don't know how big of a problem."

Troy curbed his impatience with her roundabout speaking style. He wanted to tell her to spit it out already. But he knew from experience that rushing her only slowed things down.

"You got any coffee?" she asked.

"I do." He cut through the vaulted-ceilinged living room, heading for the kitchen, assuming she'd follow and hoping she'd compose her thoughts along the way.

Her heels clicked on the parquet floor. "I've thought about it and talked about it and I'm really sorry to bother you with it. But it's kind of getting away from me, you know?"

No, he didn't know. "Does 'it' have a name?"

"It's not a person."

He tried and failed to keep the exasperation from his voice. "Kassidy."

"What?"

He rounded the island in the center of the expansive kitchen. "You've got to give me something here, maybe a proper noun."

She pursed her lips tight together.

"What happened?" he asked. "What did you do?"

"I didn't *do* anything. See, I told my manager this would happen."

"You have a manager?"

"A business manager."

"For your singing career?"

"Yes."

The revelation took Troy by surprise.

Sure, Kassidy was a sweet singer, but she was really small-time. Who would take her on? Why would they take her on? His mind immediately went to the kinds of scams that exploited starry-eyed young women.

"What's the guy's name?" he asked suspiciously.

"Don't be such a chauvinist. Her name is Eileen Renard."

Troy found himself feeling slightly relieved. Statistically speaking, females were less likely than males to exploit vulnerable young women in the entertainment business, turning them into strippers, getting them addicted to drugs.

He gave her face a critical once-over. She looked healthy, if a bit tired. He doubted she was doing any kind of recreational drugs. Thank goodness.

He retrieved a second white stoneware mug from the orderly row on the first shelf of a cupboard. "Why did you think you needed a manager?"

"She approached me," said Kassidy, slipping up onto a maple wood stool at the kitchen island and dropping her bag to the floor with a clunk.

"Is she asking for money?"

"No, she's not asking for money. She likes my singing. She thinks I have potential. Which I do. It was after a show in Miami Beach, and she came backstage. She represents lots of great acts."

"What were you doing in Miami Beach?" Last Troy had heard Kassidy could barely afford the subway.

"I was singing in a club."

"How did you get there?"

"On an airplane, just like everybody else."

"That's a long way from New Jersey."

"I'm nineteen years old, Troy."

He set a cup of black coffee in front of her. "Last time we talked, you didn't have any money."

"Things have changed since the last time we talked."

He searched her expression for signs of remorse. He hoped she hadn't done anything questionably moral or legal.

"I'm doing better," she said.

He waited for her to elaborate, taking a sip of his coffee.

"Financially," she said. "Good, in fact. Great, really."

"You don't need money?" He'd assumed money would be at least part of the solution to her current problem.

"I don't need money."

That was surprising, but good, though it didn't explain her presence.

"Can you tell me the problem?" he asked.

"I'm *trying* to tell you the problem. But you're giving me the third degree."

"I'm sorry." He forced himself to stay quiet.

She was silent for so long that he almost asked another question. But he told himself to pretend this was a stakeout. He had infinite patience on a stakeout.

"It's a few guys," she said. She reached down for her

shoulder bag and dug into it. "At least I assume they're guys—from what they say, it sounds like they're guys." She extracted a handful of papers. "They call themselves fans, but they're kind of scary."

Troy reached for the wrinkled email printouts, noting the trace of anxiety that had come into her expression.

"What do they say?"

While waiting for her answer, he began reading the emails.

They were from six unique email addresses, each with a different nickname and a different writing style. For the most part, they were full of praise, laced with offers of sex and overtones of possessiveness. Nothing was overtly threatening, but any one of them could be the start of something sinister.

"Do you recognize any of the addresses?" he asked. "Do you know any of the nicknames?"

She shook her purple hair. "If I've met them, I don't remember. But I meet a lot of people, a *lot* of people. And hundreds more see me onstage and you know…" She gave her slim shoulders a shrug. "They read my blog, and they think we're friends."

"You write a blog?"

"All singers write blogs."

"They shouldn't."

"Yeah, well, we're not as paranoid as you."

"I'm not paranoid."

"You don't trust people, Troy."

"Only because most of them can't be trusted. I'm going to hand these over to our threat expert and see if there's anything to worry about." Troy remembered to glance at his watch. If he wasn't done soon, Vegas would have to take the Bulgarian meeting.

He polished off his coffee, hoping Kassidy would do the same.

She didn't.

"It's not just the emails," she said.

"Oh?"

"People have started hanging around the stage door after my show, looking for autographs and selfies."

"How many people?"

"Fifty, maybe more."

"*Fifty* people wait around to get your autograph?"

"You know, your confidence in me is inspiring."

"It's not that."

Actually, it was that. He was surprised she had anywhere near that kind of a following.

"Things are moving fast," she said. "Downloads of my songs, ticket sales, offers for gigs. A guy on a motorcycle followed me back to my hotel in Chicago last week. It was creepy."

Talk about burying the lead. *That* could be truly dangerous.

"Were you alone?" Troy asked.

"I was with a backup band."

He was relieved to hear it.

"I was wondering. You know, thinking." Her blue eyes were big, and her face looked pale and delicate. "Do you think I could stay with you? Just for a little while? It's really safe here, and I'm having a hard time sleeping in my apartment."

"Here?" Troy's sense of duty went to war with his desire for privacy.

"Just for a little while," she repeated, looking hopeful.

Troy desperately wanted to say no. He searched his mind for a way he could do that.

The two of them shared a father, but he had died several years ago. And Kassidy's mother was a certified flake. Last Troy heard she was living with some kind of hippie junk sculptor in the mountains of Oregon.

For all intents and purposes, Troy was Kassidy's only relative. He was definitely her only stable relative. How could he turn her down?

"How long?" he asked.

Her face burst into a brilliant smile, and she hopped down from the stool, hurrying around the island. "You're the best."

He wasn't the best. In fact, he hadn't even agreed to let her stay yet.

But she surprised him by wrapping her arms around him and squeezing tight. "Thank you, big brother."

Something tugged at his heart. "You're welcome," he told her.

She drew back. "You're going to love Drake."

Wait a minute. "You want to bring a *boyfriend* here?"

That put an entirely different spin on the situation. No way, no how, was some random guy going to stay in Troy's apartment.

"Drake's not my boyfriend," she said, her eyes still bright with joy. "He's my son."

Mila Stern was on a mission.

At times it seemed doomed, but she wasn't giving up, because Sterns never gave up. She had three siblings and two parents who proved that to her every single day.

Coming up on noon, she approached the front door of the Pinion Security building, squaring her shoulders, drawing a bracing breath and mentally rehearsing her opening lines.

Five minutes, she'd tell Troy Keiser. He only needed to listen to her pitch for five short minutes. That was barely any time at all, and it had the potential to increase his business by 10 percent.

Did 10 percent sound like enough? she wondered. Maybe she should claim 15 percent. Or was fifteen too much of a stretch?

No. It wasn't a stretch. The number of women in need of some form of personal protection was growing by the month. In fact, it was growing by the week. Maybe even by the day. Should she say day?

Yes. By the day. That was a perfectly fair claim to make—15 percent and growing by the day.

Dressed in pale gray cargo pants, a blue sweater and sturdy leather boots, she pulled open the stenciled glass entry door. The Pinion reception area was compact, decorated in gray tones, with a sleek steel-and-smoked-glass counter curving around the back wall. A man stood behind it dressed in black. His hair was cropped short, his chin square and strong, and his arms and shoulders all but bulging from the three-quarter sleeves of his T-shirt.

"Can I help you?" he asked in a deep voice.

She smiled, trying to look friendly and innocuous, like the kind of person a man would want to help. "I hope so," she said, striding forward to the countertop. "I'm looking for Troy Keiser."

The man hit a couple of keys on a computer terminal recessed into the desk in front of him. "You have an appointment?"

"Not for today," she answered. "We've been corresponding for a few weeks, and my plans were fluid." She stopped talking, hoping he'd draw the conclusion that Troy Keiser was willing, even intending to make an appointment with her.

"Your name?" he asked.

She wished he hadn't asked that, but she couldn't see a way around giving it to him. "Mila Stern."

Troy Keiser—and, she had to assume, the entire human resources unit of Pinion Security—would recognize her name as the woman whose job application they'd rejected three times over.

The man pressed a button on his compact headset.

Mila continued to smile even as tension built within her. She was fully qualified to become a security agent at Pinion, even if Troy Keiser wouldn't admit it. She had a degree in criminology and a black belt in Krav Maga, along with significant technical surveillance and tactical weapons training.

The man waited, and Mila waited. She knew if he talked to Troy Keiser, it would be game over before she made it past the lobby.

Her gaze flicked to the elevator doors behind him. No doubt they were controlled by a passkey. If she was lucky, there was also a staircase from the lobby. She drew his attention by smoothing back her brown hair, pretending to check the French braid that held it in place. At the same time, she surreptitiously scanned the room.

There it was. A stairway door. She let her gaze slide right past it without pausing. If Troy refused to see her, she'd make a break for the stairway. Reception man would have to circle the end of the counter to come after her, giving her a head start of two, maybe three seconds.

He might call for backup on the second floor, but that would take five to seven seconds. She could run a flight of stairs in three, and this was only a nine-story building. She'd duck out at the fourth floor and try to lose them. Assuming the stairwell doors weren't locked. They could easily be locked.

The man ended the phone call without speaking and pressed another number.

Mila waited, hoping a new call might work in her favor.

"Vegas?" the man said into the phone. "There's a woman here for Troy. No, no appointment. Mila Stern."

He paused, his eyes narrowing on Mila.

She shifted her weight to the ball of her left foot, getting ready to sprint.

"Will do," he said. The suspicion seemed to go out of his eyes.

She took a chance and waited a moment longer.

He ended the call. "You can meet Hugh Fielding on the second floor."

Yes. At least she'd make it out of the lobby.

"Is Troy here?" she dared ask.

"He's busy at the moment. But Vegas should be able to help you."

She wanted to ask what Troy was doing, or more importantly *where* Troy was doing it. Was he on the second floor or somewhere else?

The man pressed a button, and a light on the elevator behind him turned from red to green.

"Thank you," said Mila, heading for the elevator.

She knew that Hugh Fielding, nicknamed Vegas, was Troy's business partner. He might not have recognized her name. Then again, he might be planning to run interference, to keep her away from Troy, maybe even to escort her directly out of the building.

During her research of the company, she'd learned Troy Keiser undertook most management functions, including making the hiring decisions. It seemed Vegas Fielding was the technical expert.

She stepped inside the elevator. The two was already lighted on the panel. Taking a chance, she reached out and pressed nine—might as well get as far away from Vegas as possible to start her search. The white circle lit up.

The doors closed, and she moved to a front corner, flush against the wall beside the door. If she was very lucky, Hugh Fielding would think the car was empty and assume she was catching the next elevator.

It stopped on two, and the doors whooshed open.

Mila held her breath, hearing phone chimes and several voices outside. No footfalls approached the elevator, and none of the voices seemed raised in alarm.

The doors closed again, and she let out her breath, easing out of the corner as the numbers counted to nine.

When the doors opened on the ninth floor, Troy himself stood outside. His arms were folded over his chest, and his feet were braced apart. It was obvious he was expecting her.

"Seriously?" he asked with an arched brow.

"Hello, Mr. Keiser." She quickly exited the elevator.

If it descended without her, she'd have at least a few moments with him.

"You just broke into my building."

"No," she disagreed. "Mr. Fielding invited me in. I'm sure nobody could break into the Pinion Security building."

A flare came into his blue eyes. She could only hope it was amusement and not anger.

"Vegas invited you to the *second* floor."

"But the person I really want to see is you."

"So you hijacked the elevator to the private floor?"

Mila glanced along the short hallway that ended in two doors. "I didn't realize it was a private floor." She wasn't about to admit she'd planned to search the building from the top down in order to find him.

"How can I help you, Ms. Stern? And no, you can't have a job. Sweet-talking your way past reception does not prove your superior tradecraft skills."

"That wasn't my intent."

"What was your intent?"

"To talk to you in person."

"Let's get this over with."

Mila's brain immediately leaped to her rehearsed points. "I don't know if you're aware, but the number of high-profile businesswomen, female politicians and celebrities in need of some form of personal protection is rising every year. Estimates show that companies focusing on that fast-growing demographic can see an increase in business of up to 15 percent per year. And offering services that cater specifically to—"

"You're making that up."

She didn't let the interruption rattle her. "I'm not. Any number of public sources can point to the rise in female political figures, industrialists, high-powered rock stars."

"The 15 percent. You made up the 15 percent."

He had to be guessing. Mila was a very good liar.

"It's more anecdotal than scientific," she allowed. "But the fundamental point—"

"We already cater to women," said Troy. "We protect hundreds of women, with better than a 99-percent success rate."

There was something slightly off in his expression. He

was lying right back at her. But why would he lie? And then she got it. He was making up the 99 percent to mock her.

"You're making that up," she said softly.

"Any number of sources will verify that we have a robust female clientele."

She struggled not to smile. "You're making up the 99 percent."

"It's my company."

"You've got a tell."

"I do not."

She lifted her chin. "Right there. Next to your left ear. There's a muscle that twitches when you're lying."

"That's preposterous."

"Tell me another lie."

"I'll tell you the truth," he said. "I'm not hiring you, not now, not ever."

"Because I'm a woman."

"Because you're a woman."

"And you think that means I can't fight hand to hand."

"I don't just think that. It's a fact."

"I'm pretty good," she said, putting a challenge into her tone. "You want to spar?"

He gave a chopped laugh. "You're weak *and* delusional."

"I don't expect to beat you."

Her statement seemed to puzzle him. "Then why the challenge?"

"I expect to do well, surprise you, exceed your expectations."

"You'll get hurt."

She gave a shrug. "Probably a little."

"Probably a lot."

"I really want this job."

"No kidding. But I'm not going to give you a job because you're foolish enough to challenge me in hand-to-hand combat."

"Try me."

His phone rang in his pocket.

"No," he said to her before answering it. Then he made a half turn away from her. "Yeah?"

Mila regrouped. She knew she could hold her own against him, and she knew she would surprise him with her skills. She also knew one of his major objections to hiring women security agents was the fear they couldn't handle themselves in a fistfight.

She considered simply up and attacking him. He'd have to defend himself. Then at least he'd see what she could do.

"That was fast," he said into the phone. "I'm already up on the ninth."

He was distracted at the moment, half turned away from her. It would give her an advantage in the first few seconds. His ribs were exposed, and his stance was slightly off balance.

He glanced at her and instantly drew back, an expression of surprise on his face.

"Gotta go," he said into the phone. "Don't even *think* about it," he said to Mila.

So much for her advantage of surprise. Still, the tactic had a reasonable chance of success.

The elevator pinged behind her.

It was enough of a distraction that Troy was able to grab her left wrist. He tried for the right, obviously intending to manacle her hands behind her back. But she was too quick for him.

She was about to catch him in the solar plexus when a baby's cries came through the elevator doors. She reflexively looked toward the sound.

Troy snagged her other wrist, disabling her.

"That wasn't fair," she grumbled over her shoulder.

"Nothing in this business is fair." He let her go.

The elevator opened to reveal an attractive young woman with purple hair, a colorful bag dangling over her shoulder and a squalling baby in a stroller out front.

"He's hungry," the woman said to Troy as she moved forward.

Troy looked quite horrified by the sight.

Mila knew he didn't have a wife. Maybe this was a girl-friend.

"Then feed him," said Troy, sounding impatient.

"I *will*." The woman bumped the stroller wheels over the lip of the door.

Mila could see her conversation with Troy coming to an abrupt and final end as the two of them dealt with the cry-ing baby. She couldn't afford to let that happen.

Making a split-second decision, she bent over the stroller. "Oh, he's adorable," she said.

The truth was the baby was quite unattractive at the mo-ment. His face red and scrunched up, eyes watery, nose run-ning and his mouth open with bawls of annoyance.

Mila refused to let it deter her. "Come here, precious," she cooed, imitating the behavior of her sappy aunt Nancy around babies. She gathered the messy little guy from the stroller. "What's the trouble, huh? Are you hungry?"

She felt ridiculous speaking to an uncomprehending baby in such a sickly sweet tone, but it was the only way she could think of to stick with Troy. And she was determined to stick with Troy.

She forced herself to keep from grimacing as she brought the baby's gummy face to her shoulder. Her tank top would wash, and so would her skin. She patted him gently on the back, surprised by the warmth of his little body and by the softness. He felt as though he didn't have a single bone or muscle.

His cries changed to intermittent sobs.

"Let's get going," the woman said anxiously. "This won't last long."

Mila refused to make eye contact with Troy, knowing he had to be angry at her pushiness. Instead, she marched past him, heading down the short hall to the doors at the end.

Two

Two women had invaded Troy's apartment, for two completely different but equally frustrating reasons. Well, maybe not equally frustrating, since he could get rid of Mila Stern in short order, just as soon as she put the baby down. Though, for the moment, the baby was quiet in her arms, and he was hesitant to mess with that.

Kassidy was bent over his sofa sorting through her shoulder bag, pulling out diapers, flannel blankets and tiny socks.

"He likes you," she said to Mila, straightening with a bottle in her hand.

"He seems like a sweetheart," said Mila.

Something pinged on Troy's radar. Mila's expression was perfectly neutral, and there was no reason for her to lie about something as innocuous as a baby. But for some reason his suspicions were up again.

"He can be a terror," said Kassidy. "Especially at night. It's going to take Troy a while to get used to all the crying."

"Hello?" Troy didn't like the sound of that.

The guest rooms were on the opposite side of the apartment from the master bedroom, but the kid seemed to have quite a set of lungs.

"I'm Kassidy Keiser, by the way," Kassidy said to Mila.

Mila looked surprised. She glanced to Troy. "So, you two are...married?"

"No," they both barked out simultaneously.

Drake let out a cry of surprise.

"Kassidy is my sister," said Troy.

Mila's glance went to Drake. "So the baby isn't yours?"

"No!" This time Troy beat Kassidy to the punch.

"I live in Jersey City," said Kassidy, taking Drake from Mila's arms. "That is, I normally live in Jersey City. But I've relocated for a while. Me and Drake. We'll be staying here with Troy until things calm down." She sat down on the sofa and popped the bottle into Drake's mouth.

The baby dug into the meal, his little hands clasping and unclasping as he sucked and swallowed.

Mila took an armchair, perching on the edge to watch. "What things need to calm down?" she asked Kassidy, concern evident in her voice.

Troy started to protest. Mila wasn't a guest. She had no business engaging his sister in chitchat while his lunch hour ticked away. He had a busy afternoon coming up, and he didn't intend to spend it starving.

"Or until I get used to it all, I suppose," said Kassidy. "And used to him." She smiled down at Drake, smoothing a lock of his dark hair. "Isn't he adorable?"

"You could have put him up for adoption," said Troy.

The baby was adorable. There had to be dozens if not hundreds of stable, loving couples who would want him. Kassidy was in absolutely no position to take on an infant. She could barely take care of herself.

But her eyes flashed angrily at him. "I told you, I promised."

"What a thing to say," Mila cut in, adding her own glare at Troy. "What kind of support is that? This is your nephew."

"He's not my nephew," said Troy.

"He will be," said Kassidy. "Legally, morally and in every other way there is. You better get used to it, Troy. Because little Drake here isn't going anywhere. Not anywhere."

Now Mila just looked confused.

"She's adopting him," said Troy, wondering why he bothered to explain. It was past time for Mila to leave.

"Where are his birth parents?" Mila asked Kassidy.

"His mother passed away," said Kassidy, her tone going soft and her hand smoothing over Drake's head for a second time. "She was a good friend."

The baby was blissfully oblivious to the discussion swirling around him. His hunger was being satiated, and that was all he cared about. Troy felt a pang of jealousy and then real- ized he could make that same decision for himself.

"I need to get lunch," he announced, checking the time on his wrist.

He had less than thirty minutes before he had to be back downstairs. The Bulgarians had hired Pinion Security for an important upcoming UN reception, and he needed to get the team set up.

"Help yourself to whatever you want," he told Kassidy. He dug into his pocket for a key card. "This will get you into the exterior doors as well as this apartment. You should know there are cameras all over the building." His gaze moved to Mila. "We can track anybody, anywhere, at any time."

She obviously understood. "You knew I was coming."

"We saw you hiding from Vegas on the elevator. We were curious."

"Sneaky," she said.

"Seriously? Me, sneaky?"

"You could have said something."

"Why would I say something?"

Kassidy's gaze was ping-ponging back and forth between them.

"I only wanted to talk to you," said Mila.

"And you did. And we're done." He gestured to the apart- ment's front door. "The control room will be watching you all the way out. So don't try anything."

"Who are you?" asked Kassidy.

Mila looked at Kassidy, but obviously hesitated over her answer.

"I thought you were his girlfriend," Kassidy continued as she lifted Drake to her shoulder and began patting his back.

"I'm applying for a job," said Mila.

"She means she's stalking me," said Troy.

"Welcome to the club," Kassidy said to Troy.

"Someone's stalking you?" Mila was quick to pick up on the inference.

"I don't know," Kassidy answered. "Maybe. I have these fans." She gave a little burst of laughter. "I guess if you're not dating Troy—"

"I'm not dating Troy."

"—then you wouldn't know I was a singer. I'm a singer. And I have some fans. Not a whole bunch of fans, but enough. And some of them have been sending me emails. They're a bit creepy."

Mila looked to Troy.

He gave a shrug to indicate he wasn't unduly alarmed. "I've forwarded copies to a profiler."

"Can I see them?" asked Mila.

"Sure," said Kassidy.

"No, she can't," said Troy. "She doesn't work here, and they're none of her business."

"Why doesn't she work here?" asked Kassidy.

"That's none of *your* business," said Troy.

"I'm serious," said Kassidy.

"So am I."

Kassidy turned to Mila. "Why don't you work here?"

"I'm trying," said Mila. "But your brother doesn't hire women."

Kassidy's blue eyes went wide and she stared at him with patent disapproval.

"That's not true," said Troy, wondering why he was feeling defensive. "I have three women working in this building alone."

"Not as security agents," said Mila.

Troy glared at her, sending the unmistakable message that she should shut up.

"Why not as security agents?" asked Kassidy. Using one hand to hold Drake, she dug into her shoulder bag. "I'll show you the latest emails."

"Mila is leaving, and I'm having lunch." Troy had to try at least.

"Go ahead and have lunch," said Kassidy. "I want a woman's opinion on this."

He turned his tone to steel. "Goodbye, Mila Stern."

"Don't you be a jerk, Troy," said Kassidy.

"I won't charge you," Mila said, rising to her feet and heading for Kassidy.

"Charge me with what?" He was baffled by the statement.

"Charge you for the time," she said.

"You *don't work for me*."

"This new one came yesterday," said Kassidy, holding out a sheet of paper.

Despite himself, Troy's curiosity was piqued. He hadn't seen this one. "Who's it from?"

Mila was quicker on the draw, taking the printout from Kassidy's hand.

"BluebellNighthawk," said Kassidy.

Mila was reading her way through it, and Troy went behind her to look over her shoulder.

The message rambled about Kassidy's hair and her eyes, her voice and a song she'd written that BluebellNighthawk seemed to think was about him.

"Is this the only new one?" asked Troy.

"Is there any significance to the word *window*?" asked Mila.

Troy stared down at her. "Why?"

"None that I can think of," said Kassidy.

"He uses it twice," said Mila. "And both times it's the end of a thought followed by an awkward transition."

Troy reread the note. "It's all awkward."

"True," said Mila, sitting back down in the armchair, still gazing at the printout.

Troy summoned his patience. They were going backward here.

"I'm starving," he said to both of them.

"So go have lunch," said Kassidy.

Mila merely waved him away.

* * *

Mila had managed to stay in Troy's apartment with Kassidy while he went downstairs for some meetings. She now had a hundred fan emails sorted into piles on the dining room table and had reconstructed Kassidy's recent concert schedule on a digital map on her tablet.

Drake cooed in his baby seat in the corner of the living room. Kassidy chatted on the phone to her business manager in the kitchen, the occasional word or burst of laughter filtering out.

Mila was matching the emails to the performance dates, and now she needed to link them all on the map. For that, she needed a scanner.

She glanced around and spotted an open door that looked promising. She rose to look more closely and discovered it was Troy's home office. Sure enough, she found a scanner on the corner credenza.

It looked straightforward enough, and she loaded in the documents.

"Can I help you with something?" Troy's deep voice came from behind her.

"No." She turned to meet his decidedly annoyed expression. "I think I've got it working."

"I didn't mean that literally." His frown deepened.

"What did you mean?" she asked conversationally.

She refused to let herself be intimidated by his scowl. Kassidy was living here with him, and she had invited Mila to stay and sort through the emails.

"I meant, what the hell are you doing in my office without permission?"

She held his gaze. "I'm scanning documents."

He advanced a couple of paces, shrinking the space with his presence. "I thought you'd be gone by now."

"You have cameras all over the place. You'd have known if I left."

"I don't monitor the control center."

"Your staff wouldn't notify you?"

He paused at that. It was obvious from his expression they would have contacted him immediately.

Their gazes stayed locked, and a tickle of awareness found its way into her pores. There was no denying he was a good-looking man. And masculine strength was definitely a turn-on for her. But it was odd that his belligerence wouldn't have counteracted those two traits. She wasn't blindly attracted to just any tough guy.

The scanner chugged and whined in the background.

"You need to leave," he said.

"You don't want to know what I found?"

"We both know Kassidy's in no real danger."

"We do?"

Mila wasn't ready to go that far. Though it did seem likely Kassidy was experiencing the harmless, if annoying, adoration that could be directed at any pretty young woman in the public eye.

"You've given it a nice try," he said. "You've given it a terrific try. You've gone above and beyond in trying to get me to hire you. I'll grant you that."

"Thank you. So, hire me."

"I'm not hiring you."

"Why not?" she asked.

He rolled his eyes with obvious derision. "You're stalling again."

"I'm serious. In this day and age, what possible reason could you have for not hiring women?"

"You want the truth?"

"I'd love the truth."

"Okay. Here it is. It's a simple equation of muscle mass."

She gave herself an extra beat to frame her response. She knew this was her last and only chance to change his mind. Simple, she decided. Simple and direct was her best bet.

"Skills can overcome muscle mass."

"Maybe," he allowed, surprising her.

She felt encouraged. "And don't discount knowledge and intelligence."

He squared his shoulders, not looking at all like somebody who was about to capitulate. "I don't discount knowledge and intelligence. I hire for skills. I hire for intellect. I hire for experience. I hire for proficiency. And when all of those elements are present, I then hire for strength and power."

"I have all of those things."

"How much do you even weigh?"

"A hundred and twenty pounds. Almost."

He shook his head in a pitying way. "Two guys come at you, big guys, five hundred pounds between them. What do you do?"

"Shoot them," she said without hesitation.

"You're unarmed."

Mila knew two could play at this game. "What about you? How do you control a situation where the other guys are armed and you're not?"

"I'm never not."

"You know what I mean." She stared levelly across at him. "There are times when even you, Mr. Two Hundred… whatever—"

"Two-fifteen."

"Mr. Two-Fifteen, all muscle and sinew, are overpowered by the opposition."

"Less often than you," he said softly.

Something had shifted in the depths of his eyes, and she felt the sexual awareness all over again. He'd moved closer as they spoke. Or maybe she'd moved closer. But she could smell him now, and he smelled good. Another couple of inches, and she'd feel the heat of his body.

She told herself she wanted to fight him, not kiss him. But she knew it was a lie. She'd been trained to face the honest reality of any physical encounter. Anything less put her at an absolute disadvantage.

"You're trying to distract me," she said.

"You're the one trying to distract me." He leaned in, closing the gap between them even farther.

"It's not on purpose."

"Of course it is."

"You think I can do that?" she asked, easing closer. "With you? With all that self-discipline you must have, I could distract you with sex?"

His expression faltered.

"If I can," she continued, "you should probably hire me, because that's something over and above what any of the muscle-bound brotherhood can accomplish."

"That's your strongest attribute?" he taunted. "I wouldn't think you'd want to brag about it." But his gaze kept hers trapped, and the air seemed to thicken around them.

She realized her mistake. "It's not my strongest attribute." As she spoke, she surreptitiously shifted her right hand around his side. "My strongest attribute right now is the knife pointed at your kidney."

"You don't have a knife."

"It's in its sheath. But I do have a knife."

He moved, and she instantly jerked her fist against him to show she could have stabbed him.

He grabbed her wrist, and his other hand went to her throat.

"You're dead," she told him.

"I'm bleeding out," he agreed. "But you're dead, too." His hand gently stroked the skin of her neck.

"Am I hired?" she asked.

"You're insane."

His voice was a whisper. His face hovered over hers. She smelled his skin, imagined the taste of his lips, the feel of his body enveloping hers.

He was going to kiss her. It was in the smoke of his eyes, the twitch of his fingers, the indrawn breath that tightened his chest. She shouldn't let him. She couldn't let him. But she knew she was going to let him. And it was going to be fantastic.

Kassidy's excited voice sounded through the doorway. "Mila?"

Troy instantly stepped back.

Mila snapped to reality. "In here."

"I've got a gig tonight," Kassidy sang. "It's a good one. The Ripple Branch on Georgia Avenue. They had a cancellation."

She appeared in the doorway. "Oh, hi, Troy." She focused her attention on Mila. "Can you come with me?"

"Love to," Mila immediately answered.

Kassidy barely took a breath. "You okay to babysit?" she asked Troy.

"What?" The question clearly took him aback. It was probably the only thing that stopped him from ordering Mila not to go anywhere with Kassidy.

Mila knew she shouldn't laugh at his obvious predicament, but it was tough to fight the urge.

"Drake should go to sleep by eight," said Kassidy. "And I don't have to leave until seven. I could have everything ready in advance. All you'd have to do is give him a quick bath, a bottle, and wind up his rainbow jungle toy. He loves watching it while he falls asleep."

"Sounds easy enough," said Mila.

"Go away," Troy growled under his breath. "You don't work here."

"Your sister needs protection."

"My sister needs a nanny."

"Before you fight with me, take a look at what I've found," said Mila. "I wouldn't call your sister's situation high risk, but it's not zero either."

"Nothing's zero," he said.

"There's something there," she said.

It was just out of reach, like the wisps of a dream. But

Kassidy's anxiety was real. The girl's instincts were telling her to protect herself. Mila didn't like to ignore instincts.

"You're so transparent," he drawled.

"Fine," said Mila. "Believe whatever you want. Hire me, don't hire me, but I'm going to the performance with Kassidy tonight."

"It's a free country," said Troy, his blue eyes going icy gray. "Call a nanny service before you go," Troy said to Kassidy. "I'm not your babysitter."

"It'll be easy," said Kassidy.

"I've got work to do."

Mila fought an urge to tease him, but she bit back the unwise words. She'd accompany Kassidy to the performance tonight and file a report with Troy in the morning. Maybe he'd read it. Maybe he wouldn't. Even if her work was exceptional tonight, it might not change his mind. There might be nothing she could do to change his mind about hiring her. But she wasn't going down without a fight.

In the ops control room, Vegas turned his head at Troy's entrance. He did a double take of Drake sleeping on Troy's shoulder.

"New recruit?" he asked.

"It's the apprenticeship program," said Troy, his hand splayed across Drake's diaper-covered bottom, easily balancing the baby's slight fifteen pounds.

Two dozen video screens decorated the walls, receiving feeds from fixed and mobile cameras, tracking devices and information from their international offices. This time of night, people were just arriving at work in Dubai.

"I take it this is the new nephew," said Vegas.

"He's not my—" Troy stopped himself. He supposed, technically, Drake was going to be his nephew. "There's a nanny on the way. She had car trouble or kid trouble or something."

All Troy knew for sure was that he was alone with Drake, and he didn't like it.

"Kassidy's out on the town?" asked Vegas, disapproval in his tone.

"She's working." Which he imagined was pretty much the same thing for Kassidy.

Troy had protected a lot of celebrities over the years. With a few notable exceptions, sports stars and film personalities were mostly professional. The lion's share of what made it into the tabloids was a part of their carefully crafted public image. Musicians, however, were a breed unto themselves. They kept late hours, drank and partied, and a lot of them truly lived the rock-and-roll lifestyle.

Vegas eyed Drake up and down. "I don't get it," he said. "It would be one thing if she got knocked up."

"You do remember you're talking about my sister." Troy wasn't sure why he felt compelled to defend her at this late date.

Vegas's brow went up. "Well, excuse me, but isn't this the baby sister who trashed three rooms at the Poco Hollywood Hotel?"

"She had help."

To keep the whole thing out of court, Troy had paid the bill.

"She's not exactly mother material," said Vegas.

Troy couldn't disagree with that. He briefly tightened his hold on Drake. Poor kid. This was likely to be a rocky ride.

"I'm thinking a full-time nanny," said Troy.

Vegas coughed out a chopped laugh. "One for each of them?"

Troy opened his mouth to defend her again, but he had nothing to say. There was no point in pretending Kassidy was in any position to raise a child. Why a terminally ill single mom had made his sister promise to take guardianship of an innocent baby was a mystery to him.

"I saw Mila leave with Kassidy." Vegas let the sentence hang.

"I didn't hire her," said Troy.

"Does she know that?"

"Yes."

Vegas gave a crooked smirk.

"She may not have accepted it yet," said Troy.

"But she's not equipped." It wasn't a question. If Mila had a company camera or communications device, Vegas would see it on his monitors.

"It's not an op," said Troy. "It's a performance."

"So you've analyzed the data."

"Not all of it. Not yet. It's fan letters. If Kassidy wants to flail around onstage in lingerie while she belts out pop tunes, guys are going to make comments."

"You think there's no danger?"

"Do you think there is?"

Vegas shrugged. "I doubt it."

"There. Good." Troy sat down on one of the rolling desk chairs. "What's going on in the Middle East?"

Vegas zoomed in on a camera. "Prince Matin had a late night, but he's up and around, and the car is out front of the hotel."

"Gotta love the partying spirit of the reformers," said Troy.

Vegas grinned. "He had a supermodel on his arm when he finally left the reception."

Prince Matin was in his early thirties, had plenty of money and was a genuine supporter of capitalism and an improved regulatory regime. He had the respect of his countrymen and an understanding of the West. That was a rare enough combination that nobody seemed to care what he did in his private life.

"Any new chatter about the protest?" Troy asked.

"It's been quiet enough. John's got five guys going undercover in the crowd. They're liaising with the city police."

"The minute the speech is over tonight, we put him behind the glass."

"That's the plan," said Vegas.

There were sensitivities around the podium being behind bulletproof glass, but they'd erected a barrier on each side of the stage, so only one dignitary would be exposed at any given time.

"The snipers?" Troy asked.

"Two of ours and five will be from the police department. Matin agreed to the bulletproof vest."

"That's a first."

Drake wriggled on Troy's shoulder, moving his head back and forth, and Troy readjusted his hold.

"What are you going to do if he gets hungry?" asked Vegas.

"The nanny should be here any minute." Troy extracted his cell phone and pressed the speed dial for the front reception.

"Yes, boss?" came Edison's voice.

"Any sign down there of Alice Miller from Total Tykes?"

"Nothing so far. Problem, boss?"

"Not yet."

But Vegas did have a point. Eventually Drake was going to get hungry.

"Shall I track her down?" asked Edison.

"Sure. See what you can do." Troy assumed Edison would start with the agency's phone number rather than a city-wide traffic cam search.

"Did Kassidy leave you a bottle?" asked Vegas as he double-checked a set of GPS markers in France.

Troy wasn't sure he'd understood the question. "Say again?"

"I take it the nanny is MIA. Check your refrigerator. I bet you find bottles of formula."

"She's a nanny, not a fugitive. She'll be here any second."

"Just giving you a contingency."

Drake wiggled again.

"Since when do you care about babies?" asked Troy.

"He seems a little restless."

"He's supposed to sleep for hours."

"Whatever you say." Then Vegas zoomed in on a screen. He went still and flicked a switch on his headset. "Boomer's on that job in Rio, remember? He's on the run."

Troy's focus was instant. "What happened?"

Vegas reached for the intercom to put the feed on the speakers, but Troy grabbed his arm. "You'll wake him."

Vegas nodded, withdrawing his hand to leave the sound coming to his headset. "Shots were fired."

"At *the band*?" Troy could barely believe it.

Vegas paused. "Nobody hit. They're in the bus headed for the hotel."

Boomer was at a Rio de Janeiro jazz festival with a California band. The festival attracted thousands, but it didn't have a history of violence. It had been considered a routine operation.

"They think it was probably celebratory gunfire," said Vegas. "But Boomer wasn't taking any chances."

"Good decision," said Troy.

"Roger that," Vegas said into his microphone. He flicked a smile. "No longer headed for the hotel. They happened onto a beach party. Boomer will pull in a couple of reinforcements."

"Gotta be a hundred parties there tonight," said Troy.

"I wouldn't mind an assignment in Rio," said Vegas.

"I'd take anything with palm trees right about now."

There were no windows in the DC control room, but the day had been cloudy and gray, October drizzle turning into November cold.

Troy's phone buzzed.

He could only hope it was Edison with good news.

"Yeah?"

"Troy? It's Mila."

Her voice took him by surprise. For some reason it seemed to resonate right down to his bones.

"What are you doing with my direct line?" he asked.

"Kassidy gave it to me."

Drake wriggled against his shoulder, and Troy lowered his voice. "Next time, call the switchboard."

"Sure." She went silent.

"Is something wrong?"

"I thought you'd like an update."

"What I'd like is a nanny."

"The nanny's not there yet?"

"No," he said.

"Where is she?"

"I have no idea. You want to come back and take over?"

"Kassidy is onstage. The crowd's going nuts. You know, Troy, she really is good."

"I know she's good."

"I mean *good*, good. There's something in the crowd. It's an energy, almost a fervor. This is about to go big-time, and you really do need to think about formalizing her security."

"Let me guess, you want to head the task force?"

"Sure."

"That was a joke, Mila."

"I'm not joking."

"You're angling for a job." He wasn't buying what she was selling.

"Is that deductive reasoning 101?"

"Ha-ha."

"Gotta go. We'll talk later." The line went dead.

Troy heaved a sigh and pocketed his phone while Drake kicked his little legs and whimpered in his sleep. Anybody could see this babysitting thing was all about to go south.

Vegas turned from the monitor screens to gaze at the baby. "You ready to talk about the formula contingency plan?"

Three

Mila and Kassidy crept into Troy's apartment at three a.m. after a fantastic performance. Kassidy had come back on-stage for two encores, and the club manager had already contacted Eileen Renard looking to set up future gigs. The social media buzz that had started during the evening continued even now.

"I'm trending," said Kassidy in an excited whisper as the apartment door swung shut behind her.

She scrolled through the screen of her phone while she kicked off her shoes and started for the living room. "It's mostly good."

"I'll go through the posts in the morning," said Mila.

She was dead tired right now, and as soon as she retrieved the rest of Kassidy's email printouts from Troy's dining table, she was headed home for bed. She'd taken dozens of photos of the audience and the outside crowds, and she'd add the new social media posts to the mix. She intended to get back to her situational analysis early tomorrow.

"Oh, look," whispered Kassidy, coming to an abrupt halt at the edge of the living room. "How sweet is that?"

Mila followed Kassidy's gaze to find Troy sound asleep on his sofa. He was flat on his back, Drake sprawled across his chest, eyes closed, his face pressed into the crook of Troy's neck.

"Sweet," said Mila. Though, even sleeping, she found Troy more imposing than sweet.

His eyes blinked once then came fully open, obviously alert.

"What happened to Alice Miller?" asked Kassidy.

"She left." Troy cradled Drake and sat up, glancing at his watch. "This one slept until five minutes after she drove away."

Troy's short hair was still neat, his shirt wrinkle-free, and he seemed completely awake and alert. The only flaw to his otherwise perfect appearance was the shadow of a beard. But it was sexy—made him look rakishly handsome.

"He'll be hungry soon," said Kassidy, moving to take Drake from her brother.

"He'll be chubby soon the way he eats," said Troy.

"That's what babies do," said Kassidy.

"That's not all they do," said Troy. "Don't go making more plans that include me. This diaper duty is not going to be a regular thing."

Kassidy hesitated, glancing uncertainly at Mila.

"What?" asked Troy.

"They really liked me," said Kassidy.

"She was fantastic," Mila added. "I meant what I told you on the phone."

The night had obviously been thrilling for Kassidy, and Mila hoped Troy didn't put a damper on it.

"Is there any money in this?" asked Troy as he relinquished Drake. "What I mean is, enough for a full-time nanny?"

"Eventually," said Kassidy. "I think. I'm sure." She didn't look all that sure.

Mila was no expert, but it seemed the money ought to rise along with Kassidy's popularity. There might be a lag time up front, but it had to be worth the financial risk of hiring a nanny so that she could continue to perform.

Drake let out a cry, and Kassidy rubbed his back, cradling him close, rocking her body to soothe him. "It's okay, baby," she crooned. She headed for the kitchen. "Let's get you a bottle."

Mila and Troy were left alone in the dimly lit living room.

He rose to his feet. "Is this the part where you remind me she needs a bodyguard?"

Mila didn't see an advantage to pressing him further about a job tonight. But she wasn't going to mince words, either. "What your sister needs is a proper security plan."

"Here we go," he said.

"No, we don't. That's a conversation for tomorrow. Right now, I'm taking my analysis and going home. Can you tell Kassidy I'll call her and let her know what I find?"

"What are you looking for?"

"I don't know yet," Mila answered honestly as she gathered the pile of paper. "I'll go through the photos and the social media posts, see what jumps out. Last we checked, she was trending, so there'll be plenty of material."

"Trending where?"

"Just here in DC."

He nodded thoughtfully. "How big was the crowd tonight?"

"Capacity." She stopped halfway to the door to stand in front of him. "Which I'm told is three hundred. And there was a lineup outside."

"What's the typical for the Ripple Branch?"

"On a Thursday, the manager says it's usually at two-thirds capacity."

Troy looked thoughtful. "So she had an impact."

"She had an impact."

"They'll want her back."

"Them and a dozen other places in the DC area," said Mila. "I did some rudimentary research on Eileen Renard. She seems legit, and she seems excited."

"You checked out Eileen Renard?"

"Yes."

"And you have pictures from tonight?"

"The audience, the lineup, staff, autograph seekers outside the back door."

"Do you have a list of the new offers for gigs?"

Mila pulled her phone from her pocket and lit up the screen to show him.

"You made a list," he said without glancing at it.

"Of course."

"You're hired."

Her brain stumbled. "What?"

"Temporarily."

"Did you just offer me a job?"

"You need to be quicker on the uptake than that, Mila."

"You can't blame me for being surprised."

"I want you to watch Kassidy."

Temporary wasn't her first choice, but she'd absolutely take it. It was an opportunity to show him what she could do.

"That's a smart decision," she told him.

Now he looked amused. "Not half-confident, are you?"

"I'm fully confident."

"Are you going to get cocky on me?"

No, she wasn't. "Confidence is different than arrogance. I was the one on the ground tonight. I saw what I saw, and my assessment stands."

"You think she needs a security strategy."

Mila was about to say she *knew* Kassidy needed a security strategy, but it had already been a long evening. "I do."

"We can talk about it in the morning."

Drake started to cry in the kitchen.

"And a nanny," said Troy. "We're definitely going to talk about a nanny."

Mila sat across from her sister, Zoey, beside the front window in the Benson Street Bakery. Steaming mochas and fresh-baked banana muffins sat on the table between them. Rain spattered on the glass. Pedestrians rushed past in the half light, while the morning coffee crowd lineup snaked through the center of the small space.

"Anything worth doing has a high barrier to entry," said Zoey, breaking off a bite of her muffin.

"Do you have to quote Mom this early in the morning?" Mila cut her muffin in half and spread it with a layer of butter.

Zoey grinned. "Didn't get a lot of sleep last night?"

"A couple of hours." Mila took another drink of the creamy coffee, thinking maybe she should have gone with espresso. But, man, this tasted good.

"He's hot," said Zoey, turning her phone to show Mila a picture she'd found of Troy.

"I don't care about hot," said Mila. Though there was no denying Troy's sex appeal. "He's a bit annoying. And he's definitely chauvinistic. But he's great at the job. I can learn a lot from him. And that's all I care about right now."

Zoey turned the picture back toward her, taking it in with moony eyes. "Will you introduce me?"

"No, I won't introduce you. You think I want my sister dating my boss?"

Mila's brain flicked involuntarily back to the moment yesterday in Troy's office when she'd almost kissed him. Or had he almost kissed her? It didn't matter. Her feelings were the same, and they weren't good. Maybe she *should* introduce him to Zoey.

Her sister was five foot eight, model thin, always dressed for success, and men buzzed around her like bees on a hive.

Right now, Zoey put on a conspiratorial grin. "I might be able to influence him in your favor."

"*You're* going to sleep *my* way to the top?"

"What are sisters for?"

"Not that."

Zoey laughed. "You want him for yourself?"

"No," said Mila, telling herself she had to keep any attraction to Troy under ironclad control.

"Hang on," Zoey said, studying Mila's expression. "You are interested in him."

"Not interested," said Mila.

But her sister was a lawyer, a skilled cross-examiner. There was no chance of getting away with an outright lie.

"Attracted, sure," she continued. "I'm female, and I have a pulse. But that's where it stops, and it's definitely not going any further."

"I guess you won't get him to take you seriously once he's seen you naked."

"He's not going to see me naked." Mila felt her face heat.

"Okay." Zoey drew out the word, obviously fighting a grin.

"Stop," said Mila. "We're talking about my career, not my love life."

"Let's talk about my love life."

"You have a love life?" Mila immediately realized how that sounded. "I mean, other than the dozens of offers you get every week."

"I met a guy," said Zoey.

"A guy, guy?" Mila asked in surprise.

Zoey had an active but very informal dating life. Her career came first, and she'd studiously avoided the demands a serious relationship would put on her. She was already the youngest person in her prestigious law firm to make associate partner.

"Is there another kind?" she asked.

"An honest to goodness potential maybe-you're-the-one kind of guy?"

Zoey hid a smile behind her coffee cup. "Yes."

Now Mila was baffled. "Then why do you want to meet Troy?"

"I don't. I wanted to see your reaction when I asked to meet him. He seems like your type."

"*Annoying chauvinist* is not my type."

"Rough and ready is your type. I know how you feel about those metrosexual guys."

"Only because I can't stand aftershave."

It seemed shallow to discount an entire classification of men. Mila didn't want to seem shallow. But she did prefer a man with a lot of obvious testosterone, one who looked at home in jeans and a canvas work shirt, one that she couldn't physically overpower in less than a minute. There was no particular reason for the preference. It was just the way her hormones worked.

"You also hate men in skinny jeans and cardigans," said Zoey.

"That's just good taste." Then Mila stumbled. "Wait. Your new guy, he's not into cardigans, is he?"

"Business suits. Silk ties."

"Not bow ties."

"Designer suits. Business formal."

"He's a lawyer?"

"He's a judge."

"Are you allowed to date a judge?"

"Sure. Of course, I can't date him and argue in front of him at the same time."

"But, otherwise…?"

"Otherwise, it's fine. Well, technically fine, from a professional standpoint, anyway." Zoey worried her muffin.

Mila might not be an experienced trial lawyer, but even she could tell her sister was holding back something important. "What aren't you telling me?"

"It's Dustin Earl."

"Dustin *Earl*?"

"Yes."

Mila gave her head a little shake. "Are there two of them?"

"No, just the one."

"You're *dating* the judge who approved the demolition of the Turret Building."

Zoey pursed her lips. "That building was over two hundred years old."

"That would be Preservation Society's point." Mila had heard it all from her mother.

"It was condemned," argued Zoey.

The structural integrity of the building—or even the merits of the decision—wasn't really Mila's point. "Mom's going to have a cow."

Their mother, Louise Stern, was also a superior court judge. She called Judge Earl a brash, maverick upstart with little appreciation for the long-range impact of his decisions. They disagreed on almost everything, but nothing more stridently than the fate of the Turret Building.

"Tell me about it," said Zoey, popping another bite of her muffin into her mouth.

"Are you going to tell Mom and Dad?"

"I'm not telling anybody."

"You just told me."

"You don't count."

Mila couldn't help but smile at that. "Gee, thanks."

"You know what I mean. You're not going to tell Mom or Dad, or Rand or Franklin."

Their oldest brother, Rand, was a decorated captain on a Navy cruiser somewhere in the Mediterranean. Franklin's Green Beret missions for the Army were secretive. But he was probably hunkered down in a jungle on some mountainside, monitoring drug kingpins or rebels.

Zoey continued, "And I knew you wouldn't freak out."

"True enough," Mila said as she worked her way through the oversize muffin. "I've got far too many other things pinging my worry meter."

Zoey's clandestine love life would have to take a backseat to Troy's reluctance and Kassidy's security.

"Things like Troy Keiser," Zoey said, the glint returning to her eyes.

Mila refused to take the bait. "If I don't get him to hire me permanently, I'll have to explain a professional failure to the family."

Zoey lifted her coffee cup. "If you fail, it'll take the pressure off me."

"Or the other way around," said Mila. "If they're freaking out about Dustin Earl, nobody's going to care that I've blown my dream job."

"You want to bet on that?"

"No," said Mila.

Not that she'd ever wish her sister ill. But she doubted even the infamous Judge Earl would be enough to distract her family from any kind of career failure.

If Troy turned her down, she'd have four drill sergeants

all shouting at her to get up off the mat, to regroup and try again. If a job with Troy Keiser was the best credential for her future career, then that was exactly what Mila was expected to achieve. No hesitation, no excuses, no giving up.

"I'm headed to Pinion Security right now," she said, polishing off the last of her coffee.

"Show him what you've got, little sister."

Mila had made up her mind to take it slow, take it steady and methodical in order to impress Troy. She wouldn't try to knock it out of the park in the first five minutes.

"There's nothing for me to do but paperwork this morning," she said. "And after that I have to find a nanny."

"A nanny?"

"Kassidy can't perform without someone to take care of Drake."

"And if she can't perform, she can't be in danger. And if she's not in danger, you can't save her."

Mila frowned, not liking the way that sounded. "My plan is to keep her *out* of danger. If there's no danger, I've still done my job."

"Troy Keiser probably won't be all that impressed if you keep her safe from nothing."

Much as she hated it, Mila knew Zoey's words were the bald truth. If Kassidy's fans were simply fans, it would be difficult for Mila to shine. Still, she couldn't bring herself to wish any danger on Kassidy. And the most foolish move in the world would be for her to see things that weren't there. She'd have to keep herself on an even keel, make sure she didn't look too hard for threats.

This morning, Troy had found himself second-guessing his decision to hire Mila. Second guessing wasn't like him. And he couldn't afford to do it. He was in a business full of split-second decisions, most of which were final, some deadly final.

"How did she convince you?" Vegas asked from across their shared office.

It was a utilitarian room, with a couple of guest chairs, computers, monitors, an old-fashioned whiteboard and a large rectangular work table in the middle. Their desks both faced the windows, side by side, looking toward the river.

"It was Drake who wore me down," said Troy. "I don't care who does it, but somebody's hiring a nanny."

"Kassidy can hire her own nanny."

Troy had to admit it was true. Not that he had a whole lot of faith in Kassidy's judgment. But she could use a reputable service. Last night's nanny seemed perfectly fine. Her only problem was leaving too early.

"Mila seems methodical," Troy said to Vegas, using the reason he'd settled on for himself. "I appreciate methodical."

"Do you think Kassidy's under any real threat?"

"I think Mila will find out. If it's nothing, terrific. Then once we have a nanny, Mila's gone."

Troy would let her go without a second thought. Her persistence might have seemed admirable last night, but she was just another investigator. He'd decided that a woman was probably good for Kassidy under the current circumstances, but once the threat assessment was complete, that would be the end.

"Have you set up the employment entry tests?" asked Vegas.

"No." Troy was surprised by the question. "This isn't a regular hire."

Successful completion of four stringent performance tests was required of every Pinion Security agent—tradecraft theory, technical skills, weapons proficiency and physical fitness. There was an overall 80 percent failure rate, even among ex-military members. The obstacle course was particularly grueling. There was no way a woman could complete it.

"So, you're lowering the standards?" asked Vegas.

Troy took in his partner's critical expression. "Yes. I'm

lowering the standards. For her. It's a one-shot mission, she's not—"

"Don't you dare lower the standards," Mila's voice interrupted from the doorway.

Both men turned to the sound of her voice.

"This is a private conversation," Troy said, coming to his feet.

"Then you should have closed the door." Her green eyes were hard as emeralds. "I don't need to start at the ladies' tee."

"You're a woman," said Troy. "And you're a temp. Testing you would be a waste of time."

"Then I'll do the tests on my own time." She paced briskly into the office. "It'll be hard enough getting the other security agents' respect without skipping the entry tests."

"You're not going to get their respect," said Troy. It was the truth, and there was no point pretending otherwise.

"Not like this, I'm not."

"And you don't need it. You'll be working on your own with Kassidy."

His concern that hiring her had been a mistake was back in force. He should reverse the decision. He should do that right now.

"Maybe." She rested both her butt and the heels of her hands against the work table. "But it doesn't matter. I'll still be around them."

Not if he fired her, she wouldn't.

He sized up the determination in her eyes and was reminded of the admiration he'd felt last night. She definitely had tenacity going for her. Too bad it wouldn't be enough. Even if she could shoot straight, she was too small and weak to make it through the fitness course. And there was no way to picture her in hand-to-hand knife combat. No way in the world.

"Let her do it," said Vegas.

Troy turned to stare, astonished that Vegas had contradicted him. Vegas was normally reserved and more than circumspect.

"She'll fail," Troy told him in an unyielding tone.

"I won't," she said, straightening to square her shoulders and cross her arms over her chest.

It was obvious she was trying to be tough, but she was too attractive to pull it off.

"You're going to carry a two-hundred-pound dummy?" said Troy, naming only one of more than twenty obstacles.

"I know how to lift."

"A forty-foot rope climb? A twenty-kilometer road course?"

"I can run. I can climb. I can swim. And I can shoot. Don't make assumptions of what I can't do, Troy."

He wasn't assuming. If he let her skip the tests, the guys might not like it, but that was on him. If she took the tests and failed, then it was on her. She was either too dumb or too stubborn to understand the risks.

She walked toward him, lips pursing.

The closer she got, the more vivid his memory. He could see her in his apartment office, her cheeks flushed, her chest rising and falling, the awareness in her green eyes and that final moment when she'd realized he was going to kiss her.

He wanted to kiss those pursed lips right here and now. He didn't want her struggling through the obstacle course, stumbling with exhaustion, crawling through mud. He'd seen tough men reduced to tears over it. How would that help her gain the respect of her fellow security agents?

"No," he told her in a resolute tone.

"Yes," she said, stopping only inches from him, looking up into his eyes, hers glittering with icy determination. "Can't you see I'm trying to help you?"

"Can't you see I don't want your help?" She looked to Vegas, addressing her next question to him. "He's your partner. How do I change his mind?"

Vegas shrugged his broad shoulders. "Personally, I use thirty-year-old single malt."

"Done," Mila said without hesitation.

She made a crisp turn and left the office.

Troy glared at Vegas. "Really? You advised her to bribe me?"

Vegas gave an amused smile. "You should thank me. I was going to suggest she use sex."

"What?"

"I can see the way you look at her."

"That is *not* where this is going."

Sure, Mila was attractive. And maybe he wanted to kiss her. Maybe he wanted to do more. But that was simple hormones.

There was no denying she was sexy. But there wasn't a chance in the world he'd take a bad situation and make it even worse.

Besides, he assured himself, he liked his women soft and malleable, someone with a pretty hairdo, makeup and a silk dress. There were differences between men and women. As far as Troy was concerned, the more acute those differences, the better.

Sleep with Mila—yeah, right.

Sleep with an employee, not a chance.

And the idea that she could vamp him into changing his mind was laughable.

"We'll see," said Vegas.

"No, we won't see. I've made a decision."

"It's the wrong decision." Vegas looked completely serious. "You just parachute her in, without having her take the tests, and the guys will eat her for lunch."

"They're going to eat her for lunch anyway. That's why we don't hire women."

"Maybe we should," said Vegas. "If we'd hired one before now, this wouldn't be such a problem."

Troy clamped his jaw. He didn't have to say the words out loud.

Vegas's expression took on a shade of sympathy. "We've lost men before, too."

"But not through our own stupidity."

"We weren't stupid to hire Gabriela."

"We were stupid to get her killed on day five."

"Ops go bad sometimes," said Vegas.

"She never should have been in that house."

"It wasn't because she was a woman."

"Yeah, it was."

Vegas heaved a sigh. "It was a bad deal all around."

Troy dropped back down into his chair. "It was. And I'm not going to make the same mistake twice."

"Nobody's asking you to do that."

Troy stared at Vegas, but all he saw were Gabriela's big brown eyes. She'd been laughing as she left the office that day. She'd had a date coming up on the weekend, some guy she'd met at the gym. Troy remembered feeling sorry for him, knowing Gabriela was as tough as they came.

"The obstacle course isn't dangerous." Vegas interrupted his thoughts.

Troy switched his focus to the present. "Yes, it is."

"Okay, it is dangerous, but it's not deadly. And you are hiring Mila to protect your sister."

"I'm hiring her to read social media and find a nanny."

"She's not working in a bubble. And she's trained. She's got some experience. Give her a chance with the company tests. You know she'll get more respect for trying and failing than she will for not stepping up at all."

Troy opened his mouth to rebut, but a new argument didn't form. He realized that stopping Mila from taking the tests wasn't his best move. His best move would have been not have hired her in the first place.

He hated it when he screwed up.

Four

"Time," Troy shouted, and the lights came up in Pinion's basement shooting range.

Mila set the completely reassembled AK-47 down on the table and stepped back, mentally crossing her fingers that she'd gotten it all right. Target shooting was one thing, and she'd aced that part of the exam. She was also confident her reflexes had been fast and her aim accurate in the tactical house.

Troy approached the table and lifted the weapon.

"You should have warned me," she said.

"I did warn you."

"I meant that I'd be disassembling an automatic weapon under combat conditions."

He gave a ghost of a smirk. "It was recorded gunfire and flashing lights."

"I wasn't expecting combat field weapons. Who uses an AK-47 on the streets of DC?"

"Hopefully, no one."

"Then why test me on it?"

Had she known he was testing her as a combat mercenary, she'd have refreshed her memory on a whole bunch of topics.

"You wanted the standard tests. Pinion has offices in Europe, South America and the Middle East."

She couldn't help but move forward for a closer look. She wanted to ask him if she'd passed, but she also wanted to look confident by pretending not to be worried.

"Will you send me to South America?" she asked instead.

"You don't want to sleep on the floor of the jungle."

"I'm not a princess."

He barked out a laugh. "You don't have to be a princess to hate leeches and poisonous snakes."

"Do you hate them?"

"Yes."

"Do you put up with them?"

"Only when I have to." After an initial inspection, he worked the action of the gun.

She held her breath, but the click and clatter sounded normal. Thank goodness.

She kept her voice even and unconcerned, pretending she wasn't attuned to his every movement, expression and word. "What's your main focus in South America?"

Research had told her Pinion protected business executives and provided security to resource companies operating in areas with drug trade and guerrilla activity.

He walked the few paces to the shooting range and pushed a magazine into the gun. "Lately, it's been VIPs. Kidnappings are on the rise. Mine-site protection is pretty much standardized, and very effective. The drug lords don't mess with gems and minerals, and the guerrilla groups want the notoriety of a high-profile hostage as much as they want the insurance payout."

"Kidnapping insurance has been a mixed blessing."

He snapped on a set of earmuffs and raised the weapon to his shoulder. She followed suit, covering her own ears.

"You could put it that way," he shouted.

Then he pulled the trigger, and three shots rang out in rapid succession, hitting the center of a bull's-eye target fifty yards away.

"It's better if they have insurance," he stated in a raised voice, releasing the magazine and popping a cartridge out of the chamber.

"If there was no insurance, on aggregate, fewer people would get kidnapped." She pulled off the earmuffs.

"I'm insured," he said, placing the AK-47 back on the table and removing his own hearing protection. "And as a Pinion employee, you are, too."

"So you could send me to South America."

"Bushmasters grow up to ten feet long."

"Venomous?"

"Yes."

She wasn't even going to pretend she wanted to cope with a ten-foot snake. "Perhaps a nice city posting. Maybe Buenos Aires?"

He'd come closer as they spoke. "Not a lot of guerrilla activity in Buenos Aires."

His eyes were deep blue, intelligent with a trace of humor.

He was incredibly sexy. If he was anyone else, in any other circumstance, she'd be parting her lips, tipping her head with an invitation. Or maybe she'd just up and kiss him, forget waiting for him to make the first move.

"You passed weapons proficiency," he said softly.

"I know."

The back of his hand brushed hers, sending a rush of warmth along her arm. He didn't pull away, and neither did she.

"Is that bravado?" he asked, carefully watching her expression.

"I'm well trained."

She knew she should back away. She was sending signals she didn't want to send, waiting for something to happen that couldn't happen. Her brain was conjuring up his kiss in vivid detail. He had to be a fantastic kisser. A man didn't look like that, didn't smell like that, didn't have that predatory expression if he wasn't about to deliver an amazing kiss.

He tripped the backs of his fingertips up her bare arm.

Her stomach contracted. It fluttered. Her entire body stilled in anticipation.

The buzz of the fluorescents grew louder while the white light flickered rapidly in her peripheral vision. Troy's earthy scent blocked out the sharp tang of gunpowder. Her skin was heating, the moist air pressing against it like bathwater.

He bent his head.

She waited.

His lips brushed hers, and heat rocked to her core.

He groaned, leaning into her, his arms wrapping around her, his lips going firm against hers, parting, invading.

She kissed him back, her hands balling into fists, pressing them to his hips. This was reckless and dangerous and downright stupid, but she gave in to the insistent pangs of arousal as they coursed through her. She touched her tongue to his, marveling at the flood of sensation.

Her body tightened with desire. Her hips pushed against his thighs. His palms slipped down her back, cupping her rear, pulling her close, then lifting her to press her intimately to him, her thighs wrapping around his body. The kisses went on, heated and impatient as he turned to perch her on the table.

His hands slipped under her T-shirt, kneading her bare waist, making their way up. She could feel her nipples harden beneath her cotton bra, tingling in anticipation, waiting for his touch, desperate for his touch.

"This is bad," he rasped.

No, it was good. It was too good. It was ridiculously good.

"There are cameras," he said.

That got her attention.

She jerked back. "Here?"

He nodded.

"Is someone watching?"

"Probably Vegas."

She struggled to quash her hormones, to catch her breath, to summon up the guilt and embarrassment the situation warranted. She was kissing her boss. More than that, she was making out like a crazed teenager with the very man judging her professionalism.

Maybe this was a test. It was probably a test. She'd passed weapons proficiency only to fail miserably at self-control. She scrambled to salvage the situation, seizing on the first idea that hit her brain.

"About me going to South America?" She dredged up a coquettish smile and blinked up at him.

His eyes went flat along with his voice. "Are you kidding me?"

She brazened it out, walking her fingertips up his chest. "I speak pretty good Spanish."

He trapped her hand with his, squeezing it tight. "You're telling me this was persuasion?"

She looked him straight in the eyes. "Of course it was persuasion."

"You're lying."

"Are you sure?"

"I'm sure."

She lifted a brow. "You believe you're that irresistible?"

His expression flinched.

"Think about it, Troy." She gave a careless little laugh.

He grasped her chin, holding her head still, staring into her eyes.

Anxiety overtook her. She ordered herself not to crack, to hold onto her self-control. If he knew she'd melted like sugar in his arms, he'd kick her to the curb.

His jaw clamped tight, and the moment stretched into infinity.

"Don't you ever," he growled, "*ever* try to play me again."

She'd have nodded, but his grip was too tight.

"Got it?" he demanded.

"Yes," she whispered.

He turned abruptly away, and she all but sagged against the table.

"Anyone else see it?" Troy asked Vegas as he marched into the control room.

"No," Vegas answered.

"Delete it."

"Already done."

Troy halted, relief easing the knot in his chest. He didn't really know why he cared. It was no skin off his nose if the guys saw him kissing Mila.

"Thanks," he said.

"I did it for her."

"No kidding."

There was no reason to protect Troy's reputation. It was Mila who would suffer if anybody saw the footage. And she'd brought it on herself. Still, Troy didn't want to make her life even more difficult while she was here. Only a colossal jerk would do that.

"I don't know what I was thinking," he muttered to himself.

"I know exactly what you were thinking," said Vegas.

"I don't usually let women play me."

"Huh?" Vegas looked surprised.

"She's better at it than I expected." Troy's mind rewound to the shooting range. "A lot of women have tried. I can usually spot it coming a mile away. And her? *Her.* I had every reason in the world to suspect she'd try something."

"What makes you think she was playing you?"

Troy gave his partner a look of astonishment. "Intellect and reason. She's looking for a permanent job."

"Doesn't mean she'll use seduction."

"She admitted that she did."

Vegas peered at him. "She admitted she was playing you?"

It took Troy a moment to frame a response. "Is there something wrong with the way I'm speaking English?"

"Nothing wrong with the way you're talking," Vegas said, glancing to the monitors and punching a couple of computer keys.

Troy was hit with a sudden suspicion. "You didn't put her up to it, did you? You were just yankin' my chain yesterday."

Vegas raised his palms in a gesture of mock surrender. "I've got *way* better things to do with my time."

"So do I."

"That's reassuring. The footage is deleted. It's like it never happened."

"That's what I wanted to hear."

As far as Troy was concerned, the kiss had never happened. It had been tradecraft, that was all. Mila was a beautiful woman. She knew it and had seen an advantage in flirting with him. Under normal circumstances, if she was on an operation, he'd admire her skill.

"Did she pass?" Vegas asked.

"Yes."

Mila was definitely proficient in the use of firearms.

"Care to elaborate?"

"She's good with a gun. Her reaction time is acceptable, so is her judgment under fire."

"A ringing endorsement," Vegas drawled.

"What do you want me to say?"

"She scored 100 percent in the tactical house."

"Lots of guys do that."

"And we hire them."

"Are you making a point?" asked Troy.

"What are you going to do if she aces it all?"

"She's five feet four, less than a hundred and twenty pounds. There's no amount of training, grit or determination that gets her through the obstacle course."

"True enough," said Vegas. "Your sister is on her way down."

Troy glanced at the elevator camera feed to see Kassidy inside with a crying Drake in her arms. She looked exhausted, her purple hair messy and her makeup smeared.

"I'm glad we don't have audio," said Vegas.

"This is ridiculous," said Troy.

"Might be a good time to suggest she rethink her life plan."

On the monitor, the elevator doors opened. Down the hall, Drake's piercing cries echoed along the passage.

The sound grew inexorably louder until Kassidy came through the doorway.

"He's teething," she said.

"So you brought him *here*?" Troy's question sounded like an accusation.

"I needed to talk to you."

"We're trying to work here." Even as he admonished her, he found himself taking the blubbering Drake from her arms.

He had no desire to be anywhere near the shrieking, soggy, slimy baby, but Kassidy looked as if she was about to keel over. There was simply no other way to avoid imminent injury to both of them.

He put Drake to his shoulder, cringing as the kid's snotty nose came into contact with his neck.

"His gums are all red and swollen," said Kassidy. "Can you give him something?"

Surely modern medicine had come up with a cure for swollen baby gums. Aspirin came to mind, or maybe a little whiskey. A little whiskey might also put the poor kid to sleep for a while.

"I *have*," Kassidy wailed. "More than once. It's supposed to numb his mouth. But it doesn't seem to help at all."

A numbing agent struck Troy as a decent idea. Still, Drake continued to cry in his ear.

"How's the nanny search coming?" he asked her.

"The service wants a deposit." Kassidy bit her bottom lip. "I was wondering…"

She looked sweet and defenseless in her pretty pastel blouse and yoga pants.

"No problem," he said. "I'll add it to the total."

"You don't have to say it like that," she snapped back.

"Like what?"

"Like you don't expect me to ever pay it back. I'm going to pay it back."

Vegas stepped in. "Have you ever paid anything back?"

Kassidy turned on him. "I'm earning money now. More money than ever. It just takes a while for it to get into the pipe. There are up-front costs, and…"

Troy tried jiggling Drake, figuring the motion might distract him.

Vegas arched a look at Drake. "And it's a pretty expensive new hobby you've taken on."

"He's not a hobby," said Kassidy. "He's a human being." She took Drake from Troy's arms as if to rescue him. "What is *wrong* with you people?"

"I said yes," Troy pointed out. "Tell the service to invoice me."

"They want a check up front."

"Fine. Whatever. Just find a good nanny."

Twin tears formed in Kassidy's big eyes, and Troy felt like a heel.

Before he could apologize, Mila appeared, taking in the scene.

"What's going on here?" she asked Troy. "What did you do?"

It was her turn to take Drake from Kassidy's arms.

"Me?" Troy asked.

"Why is everybody crying?"

"He's teething," he found himself answering.

Mila put a hand on Kassidy's shoulder. "Did something happen? Did you get another email?"

Troy jumped on the non-baby topic. "Another email?"

Kassidy was shaking her head.

"She desperately needs some sleep," Mila said to Troy. "She's got a gig tonight."

"And that has *what* to do with me?"

Mila frowned at him. "Nice."

"What nice? I just told her I'd foot the nanny bill."

Mila handed Drake back to Troy.

"You have *got* to be kidding," said Troy.

Out of the corner of his eye, he saw Vegas smirk.

"I'm putting Kassidy to bed," said Mila.

"I'm *working.*"

"I'll be back."

"You have five minutes," he told her.

She rolled her eyes in response, ushering Kassidy out the door and down the hall.

Drake's cries turned to blubbers.

"Well played," said Vegas.

"Shut up," said Troy.

"Do you think Mila will come back?"

"If she doesn't, I'm hunting her down."

Troy rubbed a hand up and down Drake's back, his sympathies engaged. He tried rocking the baby, hoping to lull him to sleep. The poor kid sure hadn't won any prizes so far in life.

Troy paused to listen outside his apartment door. He preferred to cook his own dinner, but if Drake was up and crying, he'd head down the block to The Devon Grill.

Silence.

He slid his key card into the lock, opened the door and crept cautiously into the foyer. All he could hear was the whir of the heating system, and then clicks as someone typed on a keyboard. He moved around the corner, bringing into view his living room and the dining room beyond.

Mila was at the dining table. Her head was bent over a laptop computer, and the space around her was littered with papers. Her hair was in its usual neat braid. Her blue T-shirt was stretched over her slim shoulders. And Drake was sleeping against her, balanced on her arm, his face tucked into her neck.

Troy moved quietly across the carpet to where she could see him, having no desire whatsoever to speak and wake the sleeping baby.

She caught sight of him and looked up. Then she pointed to Drake and put a finger across her lips.

"Where's Kassidy?" he whispered.

"Sleeping."

"No nanny?"

Mila gave a small shake of her head. "There's one coming by at seven for an interview."

"What about the last one? She seemed okay." In Troy's mind, expediency was more important than perfection in the circumstances.

"She only does occasional work."

"Oh. Well, could she come occasionally tonight?"

Mila smiled. "Hopefully the new one will work out."

Drake squirmed against her.

"Can you put him in his crib?" Troy asked.

"I tried a few times. He just woke right up again."

"We're waking him by talking."

She glanced down at the baby. "I guess I can't let him sleep forever."

Troy wasn't ready to discard that as a valid approach to child rearing. Babies definitely seemed easier when they were fast asleep.

Then she gave a grimace. "My arm's asleep."

He heaved a sigh and gently gathered Drake to nestle him against his own shoulder.

"Thanks," said Mila, rubbing her left arm.

She met Troy's gaze for a moment, and then seemed to remember the awkwardness of their morning. She quickly glanced down at the table.

"I've been working through some club records," she told him, moving some of the papers around, her words rapid, tone louder.

Drake wiggled some more against him.

"For Kassidy's last twenty gigs. I convinced the clubs to give me credit card records for ticket sales and drinks, and I'm loading the names into a database. So far, I'm not seeing any distinct patterns. And a lot of people pay cash at the door, so I don't know how far this will get us. But it's a start."

"Repeat customers?" he asked, moving so he could see her computer screen.

"Some. I've got more data to enter. Then I'll track down photos and see where facial recognition gets me."

Troy had to admit, it was a solid start to the investigation. He couldn't fault her work so far.

He gazed down at her profile, noting the cute slope of her nose, the translucence of her skin, the length of her dark lashes and the intense color of her full lips. He remembered kissing them. Even now, he could feel their heat, taste their sweetness, and he experienced that potent rush of hormones all over again.

She glanced up, looking instantly startled by the expression on his face.

He quickly cleared his throat, tamping down the desire to drag her into his arms. "Are you up for another test tomorrow?"

It took her a beat to answer. "Which one?"

"Tradecraft theory." It was a written test, and he wouldn't need to be in the room while she wrote it.

"That doesn't give me any time to study."

"You don't get to study."

"That doesn't seem very fair."

"This is about what you know, not what you can cram into your brain overnight."

"I'll be with your sister overnight."

"Shall we say ten a.m.?"

Drake began to vocalize in Troy's ear. The crying was going to start any minute.

"You're not going to give me any chance at all, are you?" she asked.

"I'm giving you exactly the same chance as anyone else. Is there a bottle around? I'm no expert, but I think this guy might be hungry when he wakes up."

Mila came to her feet and turned for the kitchen. "I don't believe you."

Troy followed. "That he'll be hungry?"

"Ha-ha." She passed through to the kitchen. "That you give all of your employees a pop quiz on tradecraft."

"I do."

She removed a baby bottle from the fridge and turned on the hot water. "You want me to fail."

"I expect you to fail. That's not the same thing."

She held the bottle to warm under the running water. "You also want me to fail."

Drake was whimpering now, taking in deeper breaths, obviously working up to something more impressive.

Troy went around the island, moving closer to Mila and the bottle, wanting to pop it into Drake's mouth just as soon as it was ready.

"I don't know what you think you'll achieve," he said. "Why put yourself through this?"

"I want a job."

"I've already told you I'm not hiring you permanently."

She looked up at him. "I'm trying to change your mind."

He fought against the distraction of her crystalline green eyes. He knew she thought this was simple. It was anything but.

"It won't work," he told her.

"We don't know that yet."

"One of us does. Honestly, Mila, save your strength. You can't talk me into it, and you can't seduce me into it."

She shut off the tap. "I don't want to get a job by seducing you or anyone else."

He lifted his brow in disbelief. "Then why did you try it this morning?"

"It was a lark. I was curious to see if it would work."

"It didn't," he lied. "I didn't give you a job." He could at least cling to that.

She handed him the bottle. "I'd have turned it down anyway."

"Now who's lying?"

She seemed to think about that. "You're right. I'm lying. I'd have taken it. Sad, isn't it?"

"That your moral fortitude isn't all that you'd like it to be?"

He doubted many people could make that claim. He sure couldn't.

Drake let out a cry. Instead of answering Troy's question, Mila handed him the bottle and headed back to the dining room table.

Troy moved the baby across his left arm as he walked, putting the bottle into Drake's mouth, wiggling it so that he latched on. It didn't feel as awkward as it had the first few times Troy had fed him.

"You're not going to answer, are you?" he asked her.

"Would you?"

He took the chair cornerwise to hers. "I've got no claim on moral fortitude." He made the decision to toss it back out on the table. "I kissed an employee this morning."

Mila didn't look up from the laptop. "She kissed you back."

"Vegas deleted the footage."

She nodded. "I really wasn't thinking about cameras."

"I'm always thinking about cameras."

She did look up then, an expression of skepticism on her face.

"Maybe not in that precise moment," he admitted.

He hadn't been thinking about anything but her.

"If the video got out, I'm not sure who it would be worse for, you or me."

"Worse for you inside Pinion. Worse for me anywhere else."

She gave a considered nod. "That sounds about right."

"I do have moments of intelligence."

For some reason, she glanced sharply up. "You have nothing *but* intelligence."

The compliment surprised him.

"That's why I'm here, Troy. I want to learn from you. I

looked at all of my options and realized you were the guy with the most to teach me."

Something flipped over in Troy's stomach. Her expression was open, honest and heart-haltingly gorgeous. And he couldn't think of anything more gratifying than teaching her everything he'd ever known about security and everything else.

But he couldn't let himself go there. He couldn't teach her the trade. He'd be teaching her how to die.

Five

In the wings offstage, Mila scrolled through the messages with hashtag KassidyKeiser and KassidyRocks. It was exciting to see them coming through by the minute, but disconcerting to try to keep up. She breezed past the comments on Kassidy's singing, her choice of songs and tonight's outfit. Mila couldn't help but smile at the female fans' oohs and ahhs over the sexily unkempt drummer.

Coming up on midnight, Kassidy was gyrating her way through the second set. The club was full again, with a line on the sidewalk outside. There were Kassidy Keiser posters on the wall, and they'd even printed some Kassidy Keiser drink coasters. Mila had a feeling that the nanny's salary was not going to be a problem much longer.

Eileen arrived by her side.

"T-shirts," she said to Mila in a loud voice above the guitar solo. "I'm ordering T-shirts and hats."

"Did you print the coasters?" Mila asked.

Eileen nodded. "And the posters." She pointed to the nearest one. "See the pattern of the purple spotlights?"

"I do," said Mila.

"I've got a graphic design company using that and a silhouette of Kassidy's profile to come up with a logo."

"Nice."

"It always helps when the talent is gorgeous."

"Kassidy is definitely pretty."

It was covered up most of the time with funky hair, exaggerated makeup and wild clothes. But Kassidy was a very beautiful young woman.

"She's going all the way," said Eileen.

Mila scanned the crowd. Everyone was on their feet, pressed up close to the stage. She was willing to bet they'd broken the fire code a few hours back. The club had to be making a killing.

She glanced back down at her phone, continuing through the endless stream of texts. Then a word popped out and she halted her thumb, scrolling backward.

A text from someone called MeMyHeart said, Drake's one lucky little boy.

A few pictures had been posted by fans online of Kassidy with Drake in his stroller. People could easily assume she was his mother. But to find his name? That would have taken a significant level of investigation.

Mila tapped MeMyHeart, finding a dozen other messages from the past hours. Judging by the message content, MeMyHeart was here. She scanned the audience, but it was dark and chaotic. Everyone out there would have a cell phone.

Her heart rate had kicked up, and her instincts told her to call Troy. But she stopped herself. Slow and methodical, that was still the best course of action.

Instead, she called Pinion's main number, getting Edison.

"It's Mila. Can someone check a cell number for me?"

"What's the reason?"

"They're tweeting about Kassidy, and it looks suspicious."

"Can do," said Edison. "Forward the tweet." He rattled off a number.

"On its way." She continued her visual scan of the audience, checking for expressions that seemed too intent on Kassidy, maybe not so much into the music.

"Hang on," said Edison. "Everything else okay there?"

"The place is rocking."

Edison chuckled. "Don't tell the boss I said so, but his sister is smokin' hot."

There was a crackle on the line, and then Edison's tone abruptly changed.

"Vegas wants to talk to you," he said.

"Sure," said Mila, moving slightly back in an effort to get away from some of the noise.

"It's a burner," said Vegas.

"The phone?"

"Whoever sent the tweet used a burner phone. But they're close, within a two-block radius, probably there."

"You read it?"

"Yeah. You want backup?"

"I'm not pressing the panic button," said Mila. "It could be nothing. I'll get as many pictures as I can."

"How's she doing?"

"Fantastic. You want me to bring you a Kassidy Keiser coaster?"

"No, thanks. But I'm picking you up."

"I've got my car."

"I'll tail you."

Mila hesitated. She didn't want to hand things over to Vegas just when they got a little interesting. But she didn't want to take chances, either. Her goal was to protect Kassidy, not to show off for Troy.

"Sure," she said. "I'm parked beside the stage door. I'm driving—"

"I know what you're driving." Vegas sounded vaguely insulted.

Mila wasn't sure how to respond. She decided to let it drop. "There'll probably be a crowd."

"I'll see you out there." He hung up.

She focused again on Kassidy, noting the almost imperceptible croak to her voice. She'd put in a really long night, singing some of her toughest songs. Her skin shone with sweat, and her heavy makeup was starting to crack along the edges. Her hair was messy, but then, it had started the evening that way. Unless you knew her well, it was hard to tell the difference.

Mila switched her attention to the crowd, raising her phone and snapping a multipanel panoramic shot. Then she focused on men who appeared to be alone. She made her way down the short staircase onto the floor, moving to the back, surreptitiously taking picture after picture. She slipped through the front entrance, nodding to the bouncers, and took in the crowd on the street.

By the time she made it back inside, Kassidy was bowing to a thundering ovation. Kassidy skipped her way offstage, blowing kisses to the audience, and the house lights came up a notch. Purely from the point of Kassidy's obvious exhaustion, Mila was glad they were skipping the encore tonight.

She pocketed her phone and jogged up the stage stairs, then along back of the curtain and down the dark, narrow hallway to the small dressing room. She took note of all the faces she was passing by, at least vaguely recognizing each of them as staff members.

The dressing room door was open, the space elbow to elbow. Eileen seemed excited, talking to Kassidy and one of the backup band members.

"Six months," said Eileen. "A trial on both sides."

The band member—Mila remembered his name was Arthur—spoke directly to Kassidy.

"What do you say, babe?"

Kassidy grinned. "I say we do it." Then she spotted Mila. "Hey, Mila. We're gonna sign a contract with Bumper. Eileen's putting together the tour."

Mila wasn't surprised by the news. Eileen had been talking about a tour all week long. Bumper was a solid backup band, and continuity obviously made sense for Kassidy.

"You ready to go?" Mila asked.

Kassidy heaved an exaggerated sigh. "I guess I have to."

"You look tired."

"I'm not. But it'll take a while to get to the car. Did you hear from Gabby or Troy?"

They'd found a nanny in Gabby Reed, who had started work two days ago.

"No news is good news," said Mila.

Kassidy slung her bag over her shoulder. "Catch you guys later," she called.

The three band members waved their goodbyes.

"Call me when you get up tomorrow," said Eileen.

"Toodle-oo." Kassidy waggled her fingers as they made their way toward the door.

Mila went first, cutting through one end of the kitchen to the delivery entrance. There she pushed open a steel door that led to a small concrete staircase. The alley behind the building was wide and decently lit, and a cheer came up from the assembled crowd that surged forward as Kassidy exited.

She put on a big grin and waved to them.

There were more people than last night, and Mila braced herself. She waded into the crowd with Kassidy on her heels. It was slow going. Fans stuffed papers and pens into Kassidy's hand and stuck their faces next to hers for selfies.

Mila's gaze darted from face to face, checking out body language and noting the objects in everyone's hands. Cell phones mostly, CDs, pens, nothing so far that looked dangerous.

Her gaze snagged on a thirty-something man with neat hair and a mustache. He was scowling, frowning at the people jostling around him. He looked out of place in a blazer and tie. But then she checked his hands and saw he had a CD.

"Mila?" Kassidy's voice sounded shaky behind her.

Mila whirled to find a large man squeezing Kassidy close, taking a picture of the two of them together.

Mila swiftly inserted herself between the two, elbowing the guy in the solar plexus, temporarily knocking the wind out of him. She looped an arm around Kassidy and threaded her way swiftly through the crowd toward the car.

Vegas met her halfway there, taking up a position on the other side of Kassidy.

"You two okay?" he asked as they keep moving.

"Under control," said Mila, hitting the button to unlock her SUV.

Without slowing her momentum, she reached out and pulled open the passenger door. She propelled Kassidy neatly into the seat and locked the door behind her.

"Is this normal?" Vegas asked as they rounded the front of the vehicle.

Flashes went off as fans took pictures through the vehicle windows.

"This is more people than usual," said Mila.

"Why didn't you say something?"

She turned to put her back to the driver's door. "I did say something. I told Troy the crowds were building. I told him her popularity was growing. And I recommended, on more than one occasion, that we formalize a security plan for Kassidy. He thought I was bucking for a full-time job."

"You are."

"I am. But that doesn't change my assessment of the situation."

"I'll talk to him," said Vegas.

Mila tried to keep the bitterness from her voice. "Because if a *man* says it, it has to be true?"

"Because I've got no skin in the game. Part of your job, Mila, is to make Troy listen when he doesn't want to listen."

"You don't think I've tried."

"Obviously not hard enough."

She told herself to control her temper. "You're asking the impossible."

"No, I'm asking the difficult. Did somebody tell you this job wasn't difficult?"

Mila counted to three. "No."

"Then, suck it up, princess. There are no awards for effort in this game."

"I'm not asking for an award." She understood that results were the only thing that mattered.

"Good," said Vegas.

"This is the biggest crowd so far." She scanned the sea of people. "It's the first time anyone's mentioned Drake. It's the first time Kassidy has been nervous. And I'll be making a full report to Troy in the morning."

"You do that," said Vegas, his tone completely even. He

glanced past her to where Kassidy sat in the passenger seat. "I'll follow you back."

Mila turned to the driver's door and used the key instead of the button, not wanting to risk unlocking Kassidy's side.

As she levered into the seat, she struggled against her disappointment. This had been a chance to impress Vegas. It was his company, too, and she got the sense that he was more open than Troy to hiring a woman. But she'd blown it.

Technically, she hadn't done anything wrong. But it was clear he thought she'd been sloppy. He thought she'd let the situation get out of control.

She slammed the door behind her, locked it, then gripped the steering wheel, swearing once under her breath.

"You okay?" asked Kassidy.

"Fine," said Mila, starting the engine. "You?"

"That was wild." Kassidy seemed more exhilarated than upset.

"I'm going to talk to your brother tomorrow. We definitely need some help."

"Where did Vegas come from?" asked Kassidy.

"I called him earlier."

"He seemed ticked off."

"He thinks I screwed up."

"*You?* How on earth did you screw up? You're the only one helping me. You want me to talk to him?"

Mila pulled the vehicle into Drive. "No. No. Don't worry about it."

"Seriously, Mila. If he's bein' a jerk."

"He's not being a jerk." The last thing Mila needed was Kassidy jumping in to defend her. "He was just surprised. I don't think he was expecting this kind of a crowd."

Kassidy gazed out her window as they cleared the alley and turned onto the street. "Neither was I." She gave a little giggle. "That was awesome."

"It *was* awesome," Mila agreed. "You were terrific onstage tonight."

"I'm really lovin' the guys from Bumper. I'm glad they want to stick around."

"Who wouldn't want to stick around? You've got to be the best thing that ever happened to them."

"They're a really good band."

The SUV picked up speed, and the streetlights flashed by.

"It's a weird thing in the music biz," Kassidy continued. "A singer can be good, and a band can be good, but the combination can really suck. Or, apart the two are decent, but together they're fantastic. It's like complementary smells. You put cinnamon and sugar together, it's magic. Sage and butter, all good. But try sage and sugar, and it's yucksville."

Mila smiled at the analogy.

Kassidy covered her mouth with a yawn. "Do you like Gabby?"

"I do," said Mila, having become used to Kassidy's sudden changes in topic. The new nanny seemed very calm, very soft-spoken, but also very organized.

"What about Troy?" asked Kassidy.

Mila tensed. Why was Kassidy asking about Troy? Had Mila given herself away? She had tried to keep her emotions under wraps, been careful not to gaze at him, attempted to keep at least an arm's length between them.

"What do you mean?" she asked cautiously.

"Do you think he likes Gabby?"

Gabby? Was Troy attracted to Gabby? Mila hadn't even thought of that. Gabby was youngish, fairly attractive, not glamorous, more down-to-earth. Which was fine. There was nothing wrong with being down-to-earth.

"In what way?" Mila asked.

Kassidy stared at her for a moment. "As a *nanny*."

"Oh."

"What did you think I meant?"

"That's what I thought you meant."

"Did you think I meant *like*, like?"

"No, no." Mila determinedly shook her head.

"I don't think Gabby is at all Troy's type. He's always been, well, a player, really. He likes women tall and blonde, with long legs and high heels and fashions straight off a Paris runway."

Mila didn't care. She truly didn't care what the heck Troy liked in women. The farther she was from his type, the better. Though he had seemed to like kissing her. So, well, he wasn't completely immune to her as a woman.

Not that she wanted him to see her as a woman. She wanted him to see her as a security agent. No more, no less. That was *all* she wanted.

"Wait a minute," said Kassidy, a trace of excitement in her voice. "Are you interested in—"

"No!" Mila realized her protest was too quick and too sharp. "No. I work for him. That's all. Nothing more." She needed to get this right. "Hey, would I dress like this if I wanted him to notice me as a woman?"

Kassidy seemed to give it some thought. "Good point. Those boots? Wow. Give me a break."

Mila couldn't help but glance down at her feet.

She should have felt relieved, but she couldn't stop a twinge of disappointment. They were work boots, that was all. She had to dress sensibly to do her job. Surely Troy understood that.

Then she realized she was acting as though she cared. She didn't. Troy's opinion of her as a woman was completely irrelevant.

Mila finished her tradecraft exam with thirty seconds to spare. She clicked the done button and a scroll bar appeared at the bottom of the screen, counting off the time while the machine calculated her score.

The door to the small meeting room opened and Troy walked in, shutting it behind him.

He leaned against it. "Vegas says you downplayed the risks last night."

The scroll bar was 20 percent done. In about two minutes, she'd know her score on the exam.

"I didn't downplay anything," she said, dragging her gaze from the screen to Troy. "*You* wouldn't listen to me."

"You want to blame the boss?"

"I want to acknowledge the truth." She glanced back to the screen. Forty-seven percent done.

He moved toward her. "The truth is Kassidy was accosted last night."

"It was a fan taking a selfie." Mila stood so he wouldn't tower over her.

"We're putting together a formal protection plan."

"Great idea, Troy," she drawled. "Too bad nobody thought of it earlier."

He leaned in. "Do it. Say, 'I told you so.'"

"To the boss?" she finished for him before she could censor herself.

His blue eyes flared, and she immediately regretted the rash words.

"I'm sorry," she offered. "That was out of line."

"I have no idea what to do with you."

Before she could answer, he continued, "But we are upping Kassidy's protection. Vegas is going to take point."

"What?" Mila voiced her shock. "Wait. No. Kassidy is my detail."

"You're contradicting me."

"Yes."

"You have to be the most insubordinate person I have ever met."

She struggled to keep her temper in check. He was marginalizing her. He was marginalizing her solely because she was a woman.

"Don't do it," she told him, determined not to be replaced by Vegas.

He eased closer, his gaze searching hers, his hand just barely brushing her forearm.

"Don't do what?" His voice had dropped to a whisper.

He'd deliberately switched topics, and her attraction stirred. Oh, no. This was bad.

His blue eyes softened, and his full lips parted.

She felt a zip of reaction right down to her toes. The kiss was coming. She could taste it on her lips and feel it in her chest, hot and heavy, a demand that had to be satisfied.

Her hands twitched. She ordered herself to push him away. She could do it. She could have him flat on his back before he saw it coming. But instead she touched his arm, feeling the steel of his biceps, the heat of his skin, the brush of his T-shirt sleeve.

His lips were on hers in a second. His hand splayed at the base of her spine, jerking her forward. She arched against him, tipping her chin, parting her lips, catapulting into instant paradise.

Man, he was a good kisser. The pressure was right, the angle was perfect and he tasted fantastic. Her hands tightened on his arms, anchoring herself while the world began to spin faster.

"This is ridiculous." Vegas's voice was like a splash of cold water.

Mila jerked back, but Troy kept her hips plastered to him.

"You're adults. If you want to do it, just—"

"We don't," Mila barked, feeling her face heat.

"—get it over with," said Vegas.

"We don't," Mila repeated, breaking Troy's hold and stepping away.

"Whatever." Vegas shook his head in obvious exasperation and moved to the computer.

Mila didn't dare look at Troy.

"You got ninety-eight," said Vegas.

She immediately perked up. "On the exam?"

"I sure wasn't grading you on the kiss." Vegas turned the screen toward her.

She took in the score and smiled. "Is that good? It has to be good."

"That's four questions wrong," said Troy.

"How do people usually do?" she asked.

"It's good," said Vegas.

"You're fine on theory," said Troy.

"And on planning," she felt compelled to add. "And in the field, and in reporting and analysis."

"When's Kassidy's next performance?" Troy asked.

His demeanor had switched to professional, remote. She told herself she was glad.

"Thursday," she answered. "Four days."

"I'll need your report by tonight."

She gave him a nod. "The mention of Drake is my biggest worry."

As far as Mila was concerned, that took the potential threat to a whole new level. Whoever MeMyHeart was had researched Kassidy's personal life and was trying to connect with her on a far more intimate level.

"I'm thinking three of us," she continued, speaking to Troy. "One outside, me backstage and one in the crowd."

"Vegas can—"

"I don't need Vegas," she interrupted.

Troy's eyes flared with obvious displeasure.

"Vegas can vet the plan, but he doesn't need to be on-site," she said.

Troy looked to Vegas.

"The guy wants to get close to her," said Mila. "He probably wants to date her. There's nothing to indicate he wants to do her harm. You've gone from zero to sixty in a heartbeat."

"You two work it out," said Vegas, backing toward the door. "I'll be in the control room, watching Prince Matin buy a new yacht."

"You don't get to dictate your own job," Troy said to Mila as the door closed behind Vegas.

"I can make recommendations." Mila didn't want to push

too far, but if she was shoved aside, she'd never be able to prove her worth. "Do other security agents make recommendations?"

Troy didn't answer.

She struggled to come up with a convincing argument. "Try this. Close your eyes and pretend I'm a man."

"That's not about to happen."

"Sit down."

He raised his brow, looking affronted. "Excuse me?"

She gave herself a beat, slowing things down, trying to work up an appropriate level of deference without compromising her bargaining position.

She sat down on one of the meeting table chairs. "Please, Troy. Have a seat so we can talk."

He watched her with what seemed like impatience.

"Please?" she repeated.

"This is ridiculous."

"Don't think of me as a woman."

"That's impossible." But he sat.

"All I'm asking," she said, measuring her words, watching the nuances of his expression for clues of what he thought, "is that you let me form a plan for Kassidy. If you don't like it, fine. If you think I'm incompetent, then hand it all off to Vegas. But give me a chance to show you what I can do. I'm just another security agent."

His gaze flicked to her lips. "No, you're not."

"Forget you ever kissed me."

"I can't."

"You have to."

"Maybe Vegas is right."

The statement threw her. "About what?"

"We should get it over with."

"We should…" Mila suddenly realized what he meant. "You think we should *sleep* together?"

"It might alleviate the tension."

"You did *not* just say that."

"Pretending you're a man isn't going to work."

Her voice rose with indignation, along with the slightest touch of panic. "Well, having a fling with my boss sure isn't going to work."

He sat back in his chair. "You're probably right."

"I'm absolutely right."

"But it would be fun."

She went momentarily speechless, and the two of them stared at each other. Their latest kiss replayed itself inside her head.

"Is this why you don't hire women?" she asked. "Because you can't keep your hands off them?"

For some reason, Troy laughed.

"I don't think it's funny."

"That's absurd. I have *enormous* self-control."

"As do I."

Abruptly, they both went quiet, their gazes locking.

A muscle ticked in Troy's cheek, and he drummed his fingertips against one knee.

She could almost hear the question echoing through his brain. It was the same question she was asking herself.

If that was true, then what had just happened?

Six

Mila and her sister, Zoey, rode side by side on a bike pathway along the Potomac. Sunday's frosty morning had turned into a sunny afternoon. Mila had a ton of work to get done on Kassidy's security plan, but clearing her head with fresh air seemed like a good idea.

"That's bloody inconvenient," said Zoey.

"That I'm attracted to my boss?" Mila asked as she downshifted her bike to start up a rise in the path.

"That he's attracted to you in return. I trust you to keep yourself under control."

"Why don't you trust him? You don't even know him. And he's an extremely squared-away guy." Sure, Troy had kissed Mila a couple of times, but it hadn't gone any further. In fact, he was the one who'd called a halt at the gun range.

"Guys are guys," said Zoey.

"I don't even know what that means."

They passed under a grove of golden aspens.

"It means," said Zoey, "in the moment, they don't have a lot of self-control."

"In the moment, apparently neither do I."

"You can't sleep with him." Zoey sounded worried.

"He offered. I said no. I already told you that. What I really need is a great protection plan for Kassidy. *That's* what will help him see me differently."

"How's it coming along?"

"Slowly," Mila admitted. "I'm beginning to think this MeMyHeart is using more than one alias to text and email."

A cold breeze wafted up from the river, and they went into single file to go around a group of people who were out walking.

Zoey pulled alongside again. "What makes you think that?"

"A few specific words: *watch*, *gaze*, *view* and *window*."

"That's creepy."

"At Troy's, she's on the ninth floor."

"He could have binoculars."

"I thought of that." Mila was going to recommend sheers or opaque shades for Kassidy's bedroom window. She was also going to get one of Pinion's technical guys to encrypt the baby monitor. It was password protected, but she didn't want to take any chances.

She was gradually meeting the other Pinion agents. It was clear they were surprised by her gender, but they were also polite and professional. A little too polite, but she supposed she couldn't expect to be one of the guys overnight.

"Does that change your security plan?" Zoey asked.

Mila nodded. "A broad-spectrum plan is different than a plan for a specific threat."

"Will that impress Troy?"

"Only if he agrees with my analysis. If he doesn't, it'll set me back."

A flock of ducks lifted off the river, quacking as they became airborne.

"Could you do two plans?" asked Zoey. "One for each scenario?"

"That'll show a lack of commitment and a lack of faith in my own analysis. The safe route is a broad-spectrum plan. The high-risk, high-reward approach is to go with my analysis and focus on the specific threat."

"If not for Troy—if you weren't second-guessing yourself based on his reaction—what would you do?"

"Specific threat," Mila said without hesitation.

There was something off about MeMyHeart. And Mila couldn't get the guy in the blazer out of her mind. He might have been just another fan, but there'd been something too intent in his expression. He might have been looking for an autograph for his CD, but he had also been annoyed. Had he been annoyed at Kassidy, at someone around her, at the situation?

"There's your answer," said Zoey. "Trust your instincts.

Don't let him get under your skin. Sure, he knows his stuff. But so do you."

"I wish I had more concrete facts. The last thing Troy wants to hear is that it's a woman's intuition."

"A woman's intuition—*anybody's* intuition—is the sum of concrete microfacts, filtered by your subconscious. Just because the conscious part of your brain hasn't yet figured something out doesn't mean it's not true."

Mila couldn't help but smile.

"What?" asked Zoey.

"I'm trying to picture Troy keeping quiet long enough for me to explain the psychological origins of intuition."

"I think your real problem will be keeping his primitive brain from drowning out everything else." Zoey affected a deep, pounding voice. *"Sexy woman, must have her."*

"I asked him," said Mila.

"Asked him what?"

"If he didn't hire women because he couldn't keep his hands off them."

Zoey grinned in the sunshine. "That won't help you get a job, but I like your style."

"It was an honest question."

It probably wasn't the wisest question in the world. But at the time, Mila had been serious. Kassidy had described Troy as a player. He obviously liked women, a lot of women, evidently.

A pulse of jealously pushed into her brain. She quashed it. Troy's sex life was entirely his own business. She only wanted him to take her seriously as a security agent. This sexual attraction to him would wear off. It had to wear off.

"Did he give you an honest answer?" asked Zoey.

"He did. He told me he had enormous self-control. He seemed sincere. You know, according to my woman's intuition."

"Then he's got it bad for you."

Mila found herself looking down at her incredibly ordinary figure, clad in gray yoga pants, a worn T-shirt, scuffed runners and a unisex windbreaker. Her hair was thrown into a ponytail, and she'd left the house without makeup. Again.

"Why?" she asked her sister. "It's not like I'm you."

Zoey rolled her eyes. "The sum of concrete microfacts, filtered by his subconscious."

"Telling him what?"

"That you'd give him healthy children."

"Whoa." Mila's bike wobbled, and it took her a moment to recover.

"Or that you could defend the family and the village. That you could skin and cook the mastodon. Our primitive drivers are our primitive drivers. We can't control them."

"I'm not skinning anything. And I don't think I'm interested in being any man's fit and healthy specimen of a child-bearing woman."

"Fair's fair," said Zoey. "You're always looking for a fit and healthy specimen of a man."

Mila had to admit it was true. "Am I shallow?"

"Not at all. Your primitive brain is telling you he can hunt and defend your children."

"My primitive brain is annoying."

Mila didn't *want* to want to sleep with Troy. But she did. There, she'd admitted it. She seriously wanted to sleep with Troy. At least she did at some primitive level.

Good thing her nonprimitive brain could override her instincts.

Mila was more than halfway through the Pinion obstacle course, and Troy couldn't help but be impressed by her grit. Her strength left something to be desired, but if he was grading on determination, she'd be getting full marks. Unfortunately for her, successful completion was all about timing.

It was a circuitous route over twenty wooded acres behind the company building. The standards allowed four hours to complete the challenging course. Most of their successful recruits did it in three.

Mila did well on the balance challenges. It was obvious she did a lot of running. And she'd done better than he expected on the mud and water obstacles. Her big challenge was strength. She was halfway up the rope-climbing wall, and her arms were shaking with the strain.

On the sidelines, he moved toward her, shouting up.

"You want to call it?"

She had a third of the course yet to go, and there was no way to make it in the time she had left.

"No," she shouted back, reaching for the next handhold.

"You're at three hours forty-two."

She didn't answer, instead took another step up.

"Are your hands numb?" he called to her.

The air temperature was barely thirty degrees. Her face was pale beneath the mud, her eyes looked too big and her expression was pinched with strain.

She kept climbing.

"Mila."

But then she was over the top. Part of him wanted to cheer, and part of him wanted to yell at her to give it up already. There was no way for her to succeed. Not now, and really not ever.

She planted her foot on a rope. Then she gripped with her hand. She moved the next foot, took the next handhold, and the next.

But then her foot missed a step, and she lost her grip. She dangled from one hand for a terrifying second before the rough rope slipped from her fingers.

She was falling, and Troy was running, desperate to catch her and at least partially break her fall. But there was too much ground to cover. He couldn't make it.

She hit the hay mound feet first, her legs instantly collapsing, dropping her onto her back.

"Mila," he cried out, skidding to a halt, dropping down on his knees. "Don't move."

"I'm okay," she gasped, blinking her eyes.

"You fell thirty feet."

"Crap."

"What hurts? Can you move your fingers and toes?"

"Yes."

"Yes, what?"

"Yes, I can move them." She started to sit up.

"Stay *still*." He needed to know if anything was broken.

"Was that legal?"

He didn't understand the question.

"Is there a limit on how far I can jump off the wall?"

"You didn't jump."

"Yeah, I did." She sat up. "That was a jump. Am I disqualified?"

"No. You fell, Mila. You need medical attention."

"I'll get it later." She tried to get to her feet.

"Will you *stop*?"

"Will you *back off*?"

"You could be hurt."

"I'm not hurt." She successfully staggered to her feet. "Will you quit coddling me? I'm not a woman. I'm a *security agent*. And I'm fine to carry on."

"You're down to fifteen minutes."

She squared her shoulders. "I know."

"You'll never finish."

She started walking toward the balance beam. Then she gave her head a shake and broke into a trot.

He wanted to stop her. Every instinct inside him told him she shouldn't be here. This was never intended for a woman. After the balance beam was a mud-and-wire crawl, and then it was a hundred push-ups, the dummy drag and a tire climb. And that was all before the final two-mile run to the finish line.

She was halfway through the wire crawl when the horn sounded. She stopped, groaned and did a face-plant into the mud.

Any sane person would be glad it was over. She didn't look glad. Then again, she didn't seem sane, either.

"Mila?" He approached her.

She didn't answer.

"Are you breathing?"

She gave a weak nod.

He stepped into the obstacle and parted two of the wires, making a hole for her. He wanted to reach out and help her to her feet, but there was no way for him to do both.

She came up on her hands and knees, then she slowly rose, the weight of the mud adding twenty pounds. She staggered to one side and he grabbed her, wrapping an arm firmly around her shoulders.

"You okay?" he asked.

"I'm disappointed." She swiped a hand across her face, removing some of the mud, smearing the rest.

She'd have looked comical if he hadn't felt so much pity for her.

"You did better than I expected," he told her.

"But not good enough."

"You didn't give up."

"No thanks to you." She smacked him in the center of the chest.

It didn't hurt, but there was a level of power to the blow that was impressive given her exhausted state.

"I was afraid you'd hurt yourself."

"Yeah, yeah. I know. I'm a girl. Therefore, I can't hack it."

"Nobody 'hacks it' through a broken leg."

"My legs aren't broken."

"I didn't know that."

"See?" She shrugged out of his grip and started walking. "Working perfectly."

She swayed again, and he looped an arm around her waist this time.

"Not perfect," he said. "But not broken."

"I'm just a little tired." She shook out her hands. "And a little dirty."

He couldn't help but smile at that. She was a mud slick

from head to toe. He didn't know how she'd get it all out of her hair.

"Can you point me to the showers?"

"We don't have a women's facility."

"I don't care."

"Well, I do." There was no way in the world he'd allow her to strip down in the men's locker room.

He helped her into a nearby company jeep for the quarter mile back to the course's start and finish line at the Pinion building. "You can shower in my bathroom."

She looked horrified. "I'm not going upstairs like this. I'll ruin your apartment."

He couldn't care less about his apartment right now. But she was probably right.

"Fine," he said as he drove down the road that circled the course. "We'll rinse you off in the locker room. *Fully clothed.* Then you can come upstairs."

"And flood your carpets?"

"They'll survive." He pulled up to the back entrance of the building.

Vegas was there to meet them.

"You did great," he told Mila.

"For a girl," she grumbled as she climbed from the vehicle.

Vegas held out a hand to help, but she pointedly ignored it.

"She's a little testy," Troy explained to Vegas.

She rounded on Troy. "Must you always frame my behavior as emotional?" She looked at Vegas. "She's a little *tired*, and a little *grimy*. And you're a little condescending!"

Vegas fought a grin. "You earned me fifty bucks."

She looked confused.

"I had you timing out at the wire crawl. I was the most optimistic of everybody."

Mila's eyes narrowed in her muddy face. "You *bet* on me?"

"Sure. A bunch of the agents did."

She shot an accusing look at Troy. "You, too?"

"He had you on the rope wall," Vegas interjected.

"*That's* why you tried to stop me there?"

Troy was insulted. "Yeah," he said dryly. "I was desperate for the fifty bucks."

She glared at him. But she had to know the idea was preposterous.

"Let's get you into a shower," he said. "You're a mess."

Her hand went to her drying cheek, and she rubbed ineffectively at the grit.

"You'd have to pay money for that at a spa," said Vegas.

"You just can't stop making the girl jokes, can you?"

Troy stepped back in. "And you can't control your hypersensitivity."

"I'm not—"

"Yeah, you are. Come on." He canted his head toward the door and started walking.

It didn't take her long to follow.

"You're going to have to let them tease you," he told her as she came up beside him, though he wasn't sure why he was giving her the benefit of the advice. "If a guy's short, he gets teased. If he's slow, same thing. If he's particularly strong, or if he knows gourmet food, or if he's a good shot. Whatever it is, positive or negative, it gets noted and acknowledged. You're a woman, Mila. It's not something they can ignore."

He reached out to open the door.

"What I can't get past," she said as they worked their way down a narrow hallway, "is that it's a showstopper. Sure, maybe it's not a strength in every circumstance. Mostly it's neutral. But around here, it's unforgivable."

"It's noticeable." He pushed open the locker room door and called out to see if anyone was inside.

Not that the guys would care about Mila walking in on them. But he didn't think she needed an eyeful.

There was no answer, so he led her inside.

She trailed after him. "So is red hair."

"And red hair will get you teased." He gestured to the

back of the locker room, the painted brick doorway that led to the communal showers. "Have at it."

She kicked off her shoes, stripped off her socks and carried them into the shower room.

He heard the water splash against the concrete floor.

"You're telling me I should chill out," she called.

He moved closer so that she would hear him. "I am."

"Why?"

"So people will know you have an appreciable sense of humor. They'll know you can take it. They'll know they don't have to walk on eggshells around you."

He realized he didn't have to stand outside and shout. She wasn't taking off her clothes. There was no social prohibition against seeing her wet. He stepped into the shower room.

Her eyes were closed under the spray, and she kept her voice raised. "I mean, why would you help me?"

"I'm right here."

Her eyes popped open. It was good to see her regular face again. Damn, she was gorgeous. Even with her hair plastered against her head and her tank top sticking—

He quickly dragged his gaze from her breasts.

"Why should I trust your advice? You don't want me here. You don't want me to win over any of your team."

"Maybe I'm just a nice guy."

"You're a tough guy. And you're a smart guy. But you're definitely not nice."

He supposed that was true. So why was he helping her? The potential answer was unsettling. "Maybe I'm trying to seduce you."

Watching the water cascade over her, he realized it was a completely plausible answer. It made him feel slightly better.

"It's not going to work," she answered tartly.

The outer door opened, and Troy turned toward the sound. "Female inside," he shouted out.

Then he realized how this was going to look. He quickly

made for the exit to explain the situation. It was Edison, and he seemed to accept Troy's story at face value.

When Troy returned to the shower room, the water was off. Mila had helped herself to a towel and was patting down her clothes. Her rinsed runners and socks were on the tile floor, and Troy retrieved them.

"Shall we go do this for real now?" he asked.

Later, as she came out of Troy's guest bathroom, Mila detected the unmistakable aromas of sausage, tomato, bread and cheese. Her stomach rumbled, drawing her down the short hallway to the living room.

She was dressed in a black cotton robe that fell past her knees and wrapped nearly twice around her body. When Kassidy arrived, she'd see if she could borrow something that was a better fit. She sure couldn't go home dressed like this.

She found Troy on the sofa, a pizza box and two bottles of beer on the coffee table.

"You ordered pizza." She couldn't quite control the reverence in her tone.

He tossed her a grin. "I hope you like sausage and mushroom."

"Love it." She made a beeline for the coffee table. "I swear, I could ki—"

She quickly checked herself. No, she couldn't kiss him for ordering pizza. That was entirely inappropriate.

"Whatever you were about to say," he drawled, searching her expression. "I wouldn't tell you no."

She busied herself settling on the opposite end of the sofa, making sure the robe completely covered her thighs. "It was nothing."

"You sure?"

She kept her gaze away from his. "I'm sure."

"Okay, I'll take your word for it." He stretched out to hand her a napkin. "But if you change your mind…"

"I won't."

"In that case, dig in."

She realized she was too starving to be proud. She reached out and peeled back the cardboard lid, helping herself to a generous slice.

Troy twisted the caps off the bottles of beer and slid one of them down the table in front of her.

"How are you feeling?" he asked.

"I'm fine," she answered automatically. Then she took a first bite of the pizza. It was delicious.

"What's sore?"

She swallowed, trying not to let the power of suggestion cause her to stretch out her aching muscles. "Nothing much. I'm mostly starving."

"Liar," he said softly. Then he helped himself to a slice.

It occurred to her that honesty would likely impress him more than bravado.

"Everything's slightly achy," she admitted. "But it won't take me long to recover. When can I go again? Maybe Wednesday, before Kassidy's next performance?"

Troy looked genuinely surprised by the question. "You want to try again?"

Did he think a single setback would make her give up?

"I absolutely want to try again."

"You nearly killed yourself out there."

"I'm a long way from dead." She took another bite.

She'd been going over the course in her mind, and she understood where she'd made some of her mistakes. Upper-body strength was her biggest problem. She needed to pace herself on some of the obstacles, kick her running speed up a notch to buy herself some more time. Then be really methodical on the climbing walls and hold something back for the dummy drag.

Troy watched her while they ate.

His perceptive gaze was unnerving, and she finally couldn't stand it anymore.

"What?" she asked him.

"I don't get you."

"There's nothing to get." She washed down the pizza with swallows of the beer.

"You could get another job," he continued. "Easily. You've got skills. You're not stupid."

"Thanks so much," she mocked, setting the bottle on a cork coaster on the coffee table.

He set down his own beer, sat up straight and eased slightly closer. "Why me?"

She straightened, matching his body posture and meeting his gaze. "Pinion is the best."

"I'm not going to argue with that."

"A topic of agreement?" She couldn't help but joke. "How long did that take us?"

But Troy remained serious. "Why do you need to work for the best?"

"Why would I want to work for second best?"

"Because it's a better option."

She shook her head. "For a Stern, it's not an option at all."

His brows went up. "Do tell."

She hesitated. The last thing she wanted to do was to bring him into her confidence. Her family dynamics were none of his business. And letting him see any vulnerability was a definite risk.

"You brought it up," he said.

"It's nothing."

"Let me be the one to decide."

"Why?"

"Because I'm your boss." He shifted, closing the space between them. "And you're trying to impress me. Maybe this will impress me. I like honesty, Mila. I don't like secrets."

She accepted his point. The motivations and psychological health of security agents were relevant to their job performance.

"My family prides itself on achievement," she said.

"Achievement?"

"High achievement. Like my mother, the superior court judge, or my father, the esteemed university professor with tenure, and my brothers. One's been captaining a military cruiser at a ridiculously young age, and the other is a decorated Green Beret. And then there's my sister, the lawyer, already on a partnership track at Cable, Swift and Bradner."

Troy seemed to consider her words. "You're the youngest."

"How did you know?"

"You're obviously playing catch-up."

"They all had a head start."

There was sympathy in his eyes, an apparent understanding. She hadn't expected that.

"What about you?" she asked.

"My company's doing great."

"Your family. What did they expect from you?"

"Ah, my family." He sat back, stretching his arm along the back of the sofa.

The arm wasn't around her, but it was close, and her body reacted with awareness. In fact, it was more than awareness. It was arousal. She took in his square chin, his softening eyes, his full, dark lips, the broad chest and firm abs beneath his black T-shirt. The temperature in the room seemed to move up a notch.

"Kassidy and me," he said. "That's all there is."

"Your parents?"

"Mine are both dead. Kassidy's mom is still alive, but, well, we don't talk about her."

"You're an orphan?"

He cracked a smile. "I'm thirty years old. I was in my twenties when I lost each of my parents."

Mila felt vaguely guilty for criticizing her own family. There wasn't anything to criticize, really. The flaws lay with her, not with them.

"Do you miss them?" she asked.

"We're not talking about me."

She felt a whisper of a touch and realized it was on her

hair. Troy was fondling her damp hair. Desire glowed in her belly, radiating out.

"Chilly?" he asked in a whisper.

"No."

His touch grew bolder, his broad fingers running against her scalp, along the length of her hair. "You're still damp."

Her skin tingled at his touch. "I'm drying."

He drew his hand through her hair again.

She knew she should push him away, but she couldn't bring herself to move. She was trapped by his blue-eyed gaze, mesmerized by the heat of his hand, enticed by his scent.

He cradled her cheek with his hand, shifting closer. His thigh brushed hers, and his thumb stroked the corner of her mouth.

She desperately wanted his kiss. She remembered every nuance of his mouth, the taste, the texture. Her imagination took flight. He'd press his lips to hers, kiss her deeply. His other hand would go to her waist, cradling her ribs, pulling her tight, or maybe slipping beneath the robe.

Her nipples tingled and tightened in response to the image. His fingertips were rough, just callused enough to be masculine. His hands were strong. He could pull her tight, envelope her in an overwhelming embrace. It would feel so good.

Then he spoke, and his voice was a low, pained growl, and she realized he hadn't moved an inch. "We have to do something about this."

She blinked him back into focus.

"I want you pretty bad," he continued. "And you're not shutting me down."

Her lips parted. She didn't want to admit it, but she couldn't lie to him, either.

"Don't look at me like that," he rasped.

"We can't," she managed. She needed him to take her seriously.

"What's the alternative?"

She didn't have an answer.

"If we don't," he said, "we'll go crazy."

She couldn't argue with that. She was already going crazy.

"We do it," he stated. "We get it out of our system. We move on."

She was tempted. Her body shifted toward him. She was inches, seconds from melting into his arms.

A boom reverberated through the apartment while white light flashed outside the windows.

In a split second, they were on the floor, Troy's body covering hers as the apartment plunged into darkness.

"What?" she gasped against the press of his shoulder.

Troy raised his head. "Don't move." He pulled up.

She sat, blinking against the dark room. Through the windows, she could see city light a couple of blocks away. Whatever had happened, it was local.

"It was an explosion," she said.

Was it a pipeline? A gas stove? A *bomb*?

"I'm going to check it out," said Troy.

She came to her feet. "I'm coming with you."

"Stay here." It was a clear order. He'd already moved across the apartment, and a small flashlight beam shone in the foyer.

"I'm not some delicate flower." No way, no how was she cowering up here while the men investigated the danger.

"You're also not dressed."

She tightened the robe around her. "So what, I'll—"

The apartment door banged shut.

"—find something to wear," she finished.

It only took her a moment to find the dining room table. She felt her way to her cell phone and turned on the flashlight.

Permission or not, she was borrowing some of Kassidy's clothes.

Seven

Troy and Vegas were on the rain-swept street with the majority of the Pinion staff on duty. Edison was inside with a few other men, starting the backup generator and making sure Pinion wasn't the target. Sirens whined, red and blue lights flashing in the dark as more police and firefighters arrived.

"A vehicle hit the electrical pole," said Vegas. "They're guessing a faulty wire, or the impact could have cracked the insulation on the transformer. Went up like a torch."

"The driver took off?" Troy asked.

As he spoke, his gaze caught a flash of orange leggings and a glittering top. His first thought was Kassidy had arrived home. But then he saw it was Mila. She was soaking wet, talking to a man in the crowd.

"Probably drunk," said Vegas. "Cops only heard from witnesses that it was a black SUV. Our security cameras might show more."

Mila handed something to the man. With a sinking feeling, Troy realized it was probably a Pinion business card. She was representing Pinion Security looking like *that*. Fantastic.

"Anyone gunning for us right now?" He wasn't particularly paranoid, but Pinion did gather its share of enemies.

"Nothing particular comes to mind," said Vegas. "Most of the messy stuff is offshore."

"That's what I thought." Troy watched Mila approach another man. He assumed she was introducing herself as a Pinion employee. "Good grief," he muttered.

"What?" Vegas glanced around.

"I'll be back."

Troy strode through the puddles, rain falling on his face, the lingering fire from atop the power pole flickering against the wet ground. The strobes of the police cars put Mila into light and then shadow, light and then shadow.

Her hair was soaked. Her shoulders were bare. And her boots, still saturated from the obstacle course and shower, were unlaced and flopping around her ankles.

He shrugged out of his jacket as he approached, wrapping it around her shoulders as he spoke into her ear.

"I thought I told you to stay inside."

"Thank you," she said to the man, handing him a card. "If you remember anything else, please give me a call."

"I'm investigating," she told Troy as the man walked away. "It was a hit-and-run. Both the police and station fifty-one are here investigating."

"But who hit and who ran?"

"Put your arms in the sleeves." He latched the bottom of the zipper.

She quickly stepped back. "Don't treat me like a child."

"We have a dress code." He eyeballed her up and down. "You look ridiculous."

She closed his jacket around herself. "I didn't have much of a choice."

"You had the choice to stay put upstairs."

"This could have something to do with Kassidy."

He paused for a moment, thinking his way through the incident. He wasn't seeing it, but Mila had his curiosity going. "How?"

"Whoever hit the pole was distracted."

"Or drunk."

"Maybe. But it's a Wednesday night, and there aren't a lot of bars in the neighborhood. Someone might have been checking out the Pinion building to look for Kassidy, missed seeing the pole, set off the explosion then took off to protect his identity."

"You're reaching." It was a common mistake, particularly among rookies—looking at evidence in a way to fit a pet theory.

"It's a theory," she said. "I'm not married to it. But I'm not discounting it, either."

"You have evidence?"

"Two witnesses say it was a man. They describe him as a businessman."

Troy waited. "That's it?"

"There was a guy at the last gig. He was in a blazer. Something about him looked out of place."

"And you're thinking businessmen wear blazers."

"Exactly."

It was the first time Troy had been disappointed in her reasoning. He hadn't always agreed with her, but he'd taken her for logical and intelligent.

"There are a lot of blazers in DC," he said.

"And somebody's stalking Kassidy."

"Maybe." As far as he was concerned, they hadn't even established that much. Nothing had happened so far that couldn't be explained by an exuberant fan base.

Mila set her jaw. "I'm going to ask some more questions."

Troy scanned the small crowd of onlookers. Nobody set off his radar. Nobody looked suspicious. He was inclined to believe this was just a random accident that had nothing to do with either Pinion or Kassidy. There was little good, but little harm Mila could do by continuing to question bystanders.

"Zip up the jacket," he told her. "And next time, wear appropriate clothing."

"That wasn't my—" She seemed to check herself. She swallowed. "Yes, sir."

His passion rolled back in a rush. She looked sexy and sweet and vulnerable standing in the rain in his oversize jacket, determined as all get-out to do a good job. What was he going to do with her? How the hell was he going to keep his perspective?

He checked out the crowd one more time.

He didn't see any danger.

He turned away, crossing the street to where Vegas was on his cell phone.

Vegas tucked away the phone. "What was that all about?"

"She was handing out our business cards, looking like a rock star."

"Why does she look like a rock star?"

"Kassidy's clothes."

Vegas looked him up and down, clearly suspicious.

"No," said Troy. "She showered, and we ate some pizza."

"Uh-huh," Vegas said, still looking skeptical.

"I'm not lying."

"You just tried to zip her up nice and cozy in your jacket."

"So she wouldn't embarrass Pinion."

"I don't care if you lie to me. But don't lie to yourself."

"She's hot," said Troy. "She's sizzling. If she offers, I won't say no." He set his jaw, letting his expression serve as a challenge to Vegas.

"I couldn't care less about your personal life," said Vegas. "Just don't make stupid decisions when it comes to Pinion."

"You think she'd sue?" Troy's gaze moved back to Mila. He couldn't imagine her claiming sexual harassment.

"I'm not talking about a lawsuit." Vegas sounded disgusted. "I'm talking about you rejecting a good employee because you can't see past your own lust."

"She's a woman," said Troy.

His decision had nothing to do with her being attractive or not. Though she was intensely and incredibly beautiful. He watched the play of light on her face as she spoke. Her skin was creamy smooth, her eyes a deep green that seemed to go on forever, and her lips were plump, ripe and kissable.

He should have kissed her when he had the chance. If he'd kissed her hard enough, maybe they wouldn't even have seen the explosion.

"Troy?" came Kassidy's questioning voice, approaching them.

Drake was in her arms in a yellow raincoat. They'd obviously just arrived home.

"What happened?" she asked, looking around.

Troy couldn't help but smile at his nephew. The hood was

askew, and Drake was chewing on the plastic sleeve. His cheeks were plump and pink, and his eyes took in the chaotic scene of flashing lights and bustling bodies.

"Blown transformer," said Troy. "It was quite spectacular."

Though he wasn't buying into Mila's theory, he couldn't help glancing around. He'd be more comfortable if Kassidy and Drake were inside.

"The generator's running," he told her. "You should take him in and warm him up."

Mila appeared. "Have you got a minute?" she asked Kassidy.

"No, she doesn't," said Troy. The last thing he needed was Mila frightening or upsetting his sister. "Drake needs to get to bed."

Both women looked at him in obvious surprise.

"What? I can't know his routine?"

"It'll just take a minute," Mila said to Kassidy.

"She doesn't have a minute," said Troy. "And I need to talk to you. Vegas, can you take Kassidy and Drake upstairs?"

Kassidy's surprised glance went to Vegas. She looked decidedly uncomfortable. Troy guessed she knew Vegas wasn't her biggest fan. Too bad. Not everybody could adore her. Troy needed some time alone with Mila.

"Sure," said Vegas.

"I can take her upstairs," said Mila.

"I need you here," said Troy; his look told her to keep quiet and agree.

She opened her mouth, but he didn't let her get in another word. He grasped her by the arm and turned her away, walking her across the street.

"Don't forget I'm your boss," he said close to her ear.

"So, I'm hired?" Her retort was sharp and saucy.

"Temporarily." He let go of her arm, weaving between two police cars to the perimeter of the hubbub.

She kept pace. "You're overbearing, you know that?"

"I don't need you upsetting Kassidy."

"I'm not going to upset her."

"She doesn't need to hear your theory."

They made it past the emergency lights and into the shadows of the dark buildings.

He halted and turned to face her, slammed immediately by a wall of desire. His hormones might have gone dormant there for a while, but they were now waking up to the moments before the explosion.

"I was only going to ask her some questions," said Mila. "Jeez, Troy, give me a little credit. My theory is my theory. I'm pursuing it. But I'm not going to freak Kassidy out for no reason."

Troy knew she was talking. Her gorgeous lips were moving. But his brain had stopped making out the words.

She paused. "Troy?"

"We need to talk about this." It was getting worse. He could barely focus around her.

"We *are* talking about this."

"Not that. The other."

She seemed to regroup. "You mean sex?"

"I mean us. You and me, and how we're reacting to each other."

"We need to ignore that."

"You think that's the answer?" It sure wasn't his answer. He'd been trying to ignore it for days. Ignoring it only made it worse.

"I do," she said.

"It's not working."

"So we make it work. We're rational adults."

He wasn't so sure about the rational part. He took a step closer to her. "We were ready to tear each other's clothes off."

"But we didn't."

"Only because something blew up."

"I take that as a sign."

"You don't believe in signs."

She flexed the slightest smile. "True. But we were lucky. Another couple of minutes…"

Another couple of minutes, and Troy would have felt extremely lucky.

"We can't give in," she said. "It would be bad for you, and it would be really bad for me."

He started to argue, but she kept on talking.

"I need you to have confidence in me, to see me as a fellow professional, one of the guys."

"I'm never going to see you as one of the guys."

"Not if you see me naked."

A vision flashed through Troy's brain, Mila naked on his bed. "Too late."

She drew back in obvious surprise.

"In my imagination," he clarified. "I've seen you in my imagination."

"Well, *stop*."

"It's not that easy."

"Then it's a good thing you have self-control."

"You're saying no." He didn't like it, but he had to accept it.

"Yes. No. I'm saying no."

"But you weren't back there." For some reason, he needed to hear it. "I saw your expression. That was a yes in my apartment."

Silence stretched between them. The shouts of the firefighters and the lights of the accident scene seemed to fade.

When she finally spoke, her voice was low. Standing in the drizzling rain, she looked more vulnerable and desirable than ever. "Back there. Yes, it was a yes."

Troy wanted to drag her into his arms. He wanted to hold her tight then carry her back to his room, where he'd strip off her clothes and kiss every inch of her delectable body.

There was no way on earth he was ever going to think of her as one of the guys.

"I don't know where we go from here," he said.

She squared her shoulders. "We go back to work."

"And pretend it never happened?"

"It's the only thing that will work."

"That's not going to work, Mila."

It was never going to work.

Zoey hung her big shoulder bag on the back of the maple dining chair Sunday morning, plunking down across the table from Mila.

She glanced around the upscale family restaurant. "What are we doing here?"

"A muffin isn't going to cut it today," said Mila, closing her menu, having decided on a Southwestern omelet and wheat toast.

"You need comfort food? Pancakes? What happened? What's going on?"

Mila briefly considered the merits of pancakes. Carb loading wouldn't be the worst idea in the world.

"I'm having a do-over on the obstacle course today."

"Oh." Zoey drew out the word in a dire tone. Then she leaned forward. "I thought you might want to talk about the hunky boss."

"I don't."

"Will he be there?"

"He was last time," said Mila. "But I asked Vegas if he could supervise."

"What's going on with that?"

"Vegas?" Nothing was going on with Vegas. He was a decent guy, loyal to Troy, sure. But he didn't seem to have the same chauvinistic tendencies.

"Not Vegas. The boss."

"I've been staying out of his way since Wednesday night."

Zoey said she understood Mila's hesitation but, like Troy, she had wondered aloud about the practicality of bottling up their desire.

"How's that working?" Zoey asked. "Have your feelings changed at all?"

Mila wished she could say they had. But they were intensifying. Even seeing Troy from a distance made her heart beat faster, her knees go weak and her lips tingle with anticipation.

"I'll get over it."

Her sister gave a shake of her head and a disbelieving smile. "That's not the way it works."

"It will be this time."

Zoey gave a roll of her eyes. "Are you coming to Mom and Dad's next weekend?"

Mila cringed. She'd forgotten about the upcoming family dinner. Her brother Rand had arranged a video conference from the ship, so it was a mandatory invitation. She'd have to find the time.

"I thought I'd bring Dustin along," said Zoey.

"Very funny."

"I'm serious."

"No, you're not."

"Rand will help calm Mom down. We know Dad'll be no help in that."

"Are you actually serious?"

"I want to get it over with. The subterfuge is killing me."

"You don't like lying."

"I'm not exactly lying. But I'm leaving out volumes of information. And, yes, I hate it. I want to be honest and up front with myself and everyone else. Dustin's a fantastic guy, and I refuse to treat him like some shameful secret."

"He knows what's going to happen?"

Zoey rolled her eyes. "Yes, baby sister, he has met our mother."

Mila coughed out a laugh. "He must really like you."

Her sister's expression sobered. "He says he does. He sure acts like he does."

"If he's willing to brave Judge Stern, he must have it bad."

"I know I have it bad."

Mila considered Zoey's admission. She couldn't help wonder how it would feel to truly fall for someone.

She thought of Troy. But that was just lust. Aside from his good looks, intellect, work ethic and all-around sexiness, he was really quite annoying. She was under no illusion that her feelings for him were anything more noble than physical desire.

That being true, perhaps it *was* something she could get out of her system. Maybe sleeping with him wasn't the worst idea in the world. Perhaps he'd be a mediocre lover, and with that attraction off the table, he'd be just another guy to her. Maybe if she slept with him, she'd be able to focus on her work.

She realized Zoey was watching her with curiosity.

"Is this a happily-ever-after thing?" she asked, putting herself back on topic.

"I don't know." Zoey smiled. "I'm not ruling anything out."

"Wow. Maybe don't tell that to Mom up front."

Zoey laughed as the waitress arrived to pour coffee and take their order.

Mila decided to add a couple of pancakes, while Zoey stuck with a grainy muffin and coffee. The young woman walked away.

"Mom can't throw Dustin in jail or anything, can she?" asked Mila.

Zoey tore open a packet of artificial sweetener. "I like to think our judicial system has checks and balances against that."

"You *like to think*? You're a lawyer. Shouldn't you be certain?"

"I'm pretty certain. But, you know, well, there's always a chance of an unexpected verdict."

Mila tried to decide if her sister was joking because she wasn't concerned, or if she was covering up her worry with humor. It could go either way.

"What time do you do the obstacle course?" Zoey asked.

"Eleven. I'm going straight there from here."

"Think you'll make it this time?"

"I don't know. It's really tough, but I have a plan. And I know where I went wrong last time."

"If you finish, will he hire you?"

"I wish. It's more like if I don't, he definitely won't hire me. If I finish, I take away one of his reasons to turn me down."

"You know his other reasons?"

"Main one is that he doesn't like women." Mila realized how that sounded. "I mean, he likes women. But he seems to think they're more decorative than functional."

Zoey canted her head to one side, wrinkling her nose. "I wonder what he sees in you."

Mila tried not to be insulted. "Thanks a ton."

"We both know you're far more functional than decorative. And I've checked the man out on social media. His dates are all glam bombshells."

"My abs are better than theirs." Even as she spoke, Mila didn't know why she was arguing. She had no desire to be decorative.

"If you like a six-pack on a woman."

"I don't have a six-pack. They're healthy, that's all. I'm in shape." She lifted her coffee cup. "Maybe I'm his walk on the wild side."

"It doesn't fit the pattern."

"There doesn't have to be a pattern."

"There's always a pattern."

"Then what's your theory?" Mila challenged. "Why is he propositioning ugly little me?"

"Stop pretending to be insulted. If you wanted to be a bombshell, you'd wear makeup, buy some nice clothes, put on some heels. You know you could do it if you wanted to."

"I don't want to." Mila assured herself it was true. The last thing she wanted was for Troy to think she was pretty.

"I'll help. Anytime you want a makeover, just holler."

"I don't—"

"Hey, that'd be fun. Glam you up, throw him off balance, send the guy for a loop."

"I'd feel like a fraud. It would run counter to everything I'm trying to accomplish."

"I didn't say it would be smart. I said it would be fun. How about this? If you get to a point where you are absolutely *positive* there is no way *on earth* he's *ever* going to hire you, we do it."

"No."

"Give me a yes, sister."

"What would be the point?"

"Satisfaction."

"Wouldn't it just reinforce his belief that women are different after all?"

"You're not listening. It's a parting shot, justice, revenge—call it whatever you like. It'll keep him awake at night."

"You're really not a nice person."

"And for all your tough-girl act, you can be a real doormat."

"Excuse me?"

"Have a plan, baby sister. If it all goes bad, have a final move in your hip pocket that will give you some measure of satisfaction."

"Is that what you do?"

"Yes."

"And if Mom won't accept Dustin?"

"I'm not there yet. I'm nowhere near there yet. She will." Zoey paused, uncertainty clouding her eyes. "Eventually."

Mila was hit with a wave of guilt. "I'm sorry. That was a thoughtless comparison. What I meant is that I'm not there with Pinion Security, either. I'm a long, long way from giving up."

This wasn't about Troy. It was about a job, her career, her

professional success. Troy was simply the manifestation of her current challenge. She'd rise to it. A Stern always did.

Troy didn't feel a single scrap of satisfaction seeing Mila fail a second time on the obstacle course. Watching through the security monitor, via the cameras positioned around the course, he shouldn't have been pulling for her, but he was. Intellectually, he knew she'd have used her success as another argument in her quest for a permanent job. And he didn't want that.

But emotionally, he'd been with her on the run, through the mud, along the balance beam and over the wall. She'd made it farther this time, but she was still a long way from completion.

He assumed she'd come upstairs to shower, so he waited in the apartment. Kassidy was in her room, taking her own nap while Drake took his. He and Mila wouldn't be completely alone, but he would take what he could get. She'd been avoiding him for days now, as if she needed to put an exclamation point on her refusal to take their physical relationship any further.

He got it.

She was off-limits.

That didn't mean they couldn't have a conversation. For a woman who claimed to want a permanent job, she had a funny was of relating to the boss.

He parked himself in the living room, where he'd hear her knock. He surfed through some news channels, then picked up a technology magazine. He checked his watch, wondering what was taking her so long.

Finally, he called the control room to see if she was on her way.

The staff member on duty reported that Mila had returned from the obstacle course with Vegas. They'd gone into the locker room and hadn't yet come out.

Troy checked his watch again. More than half an hour had gone by. Why were they still in the locker room?

And then it hit him. Perhaps she'd been hurt. Maybe Vegas was administering first aid. She could have cut herself on the barbed wire in the mud crawl. Maybe she'd injured an ankle jumping off the rope wall. She could have dislocated a finger or gashed her arm. He'd seen all of those things and more happen on the obstacle course.

He was out the door and down the hall in a flash. He didn't have the patience to wait for the elevator. Instead, he bounded down the stairs, coming out on the main floor on the back side of the building. From there, it was a short trot to the locker room.

One of the security agents was coming through the door.

"Female inside," he warned Troy.

"She okay?" asked Troy.

"In the shower." The man grinned and waggled his brows.

Troy nearly slammed him into the wall.

But that would take time, and he wanted to find out what was going on.

He breezed through the door. A second staff member was washing his hands.

"Where is she?" Troy barked.

The man jammed his thumb toward the back of the facility.

As he walked, Troy could hear the shower running.

She was in the shower. She might be fully dressed, but he had a terrible feeling she wasn't. She was making a statement. She wanted to be one of the guys. No more showering in the boss's bathroom—she was going all out.

He rounded the corner and nearly plowed straight into Vegas.

Vegas stood, arms over his chest, feet planted apart in front of the shower room doorway.

"That's as far as you go," he said to Troy.

"Don't tell me she's—"

"Naked? Yeah, she's naked."

Troy took a step forward, ready to give Mila a piece of his mind.

"Oh, no, you don't," said Vegas.

Troy stopped himself. "Has she lost her mind?"

"The guys aren't going to bother her," said Vegas. "But just in case anyone's tempted, I thought I'd stick around."

"She could have come upstairs. She knows she should have come upstairs."

"You saw?" asked Vegas.

Troy hesitated over his answer, not wild about Vegas knowing he'd monitored her attempt. "I saw."

"She's disappointed."

"I know."

The security cameras monitored from a distance, but when the buzzer rang, her body language was pretty telling.

"I doubt she wants to talk to you."

"She wants to talk to *you*?" Troy knew he sounded jealous, but he didn't particularly care.

"I'm not talking to her," Vegas offered easily.

"Were you? Did you? What did she say?"

"She wants to try again."

Troy felt some of the tension leave his body.

She wasn't hurt. She wasn't demoralized. She was just as feisty as ever.

"There's no point," he said.

"Maybe not," said Vegas. "But she won't get any static from me."

Troy stood up a little taller. "You think I'm giving her static?"

"You do spend a lot of time telling her what she can't do."

"Well, she can't do that. It's not humanly possible."

"Hey!" came Mila's voice over the shower spray. "I can hear you talking."

Troy winced, and he did an immediate recap of the conversation. Had he been insulting?

Vegas smirked.

"Shut up," said Troy in an undertone.

"Go away," said Mila.

"Come out here," said Troy.

"I'm busy."

"I need to talk to you about Kassidy." It was partially true.

It took Mila a moment to answer. "Fine."

The water shut off.

Troy looked to Vegas. "You can go guard the main door now. Don't let anyone else in."

"I don't think so."

"There's nobody left but me."

"You're the guy I'm guarding her against."

"Give me a break." Troy raised his voice. "Mila? Okay if Vegas leaves?"

"Up to him."

Vegas didn't move.

"He thinks I might try something."

"Not and live," she called back.

Vegas grinned.

"She says she can take care of herself," said Troy.

"I believe she can. Watch yourself."

"I'm not going to try anything."

"You'll want to. I'm just sayin' don't do it."

"Go away. As far as I'm concerned, she's one of the guys."

"Uh-huh." Vegas's voice dripped skepticism as he walked away.

Mila appeared in the doorway, her hair soaking wet, her bare shoulders covered in droplets, and a big towel covering her from chest to knees.

"What about Kassidy?" she asked.

Troy had to clear his throat.

"She's okay, right?" asked Mila.

"She's taking a nap."

Mila smiled, her sparkling eyes and the glimpse of her white teeth turning him on. "That's our girl."

He forced himself to concentrate. "I need an update."

"On?"

"On everything. Your investigation. The current security plan. Her upcoming performances. Anything you believe might be relevant."

"No problem." Mila crossed to a bench that held her wet clothes.

"How did those get out here?" He was trying to picture the logistics of her in the shower and Vegas in the doorway, and who knew who else coming and going.

"Vegas," she said.

"He saw you naked?"

"What if he did?"

Troy was advancing on her before he had time to think it through. "Tell me he didn't."

She met his hard gaze. "He didn't. He reached his hand around the doorway and I gave him my clothes."

"Are you sure he didn't peek?" Troy couldn't help but think, for himself, it would have taken ethics of steel to keep his eyes averted.

"Is this junior high? Of course he didn't peek. And the world wouldn't have come tumbling down if he had."

"Is that a yes or a no?"

"That's a mind your own business, Troy Keiser."

The color was high in her cheeks, and he was suddenly, blindingly reminded that she was naked under the towel.

Vegas had been right. Troy wanted to try something. He desperately and absolutely wanted to try something.

He curled his hands into fists and forced himself to take a step back.

"Get dressed," he managed through the roaring in his ears. "Meet me upstairs."

Eight

Mila had been smarter this time. She'd packed a change of clothes and another pair of boots in a duffel bag, knowing what she'd look like at the end of the obstacle course.

She stepped into her jeans and tugged a rust-colored T-shirt over her head. Her leather ankle boots were scuffed and worn, but they fit her like a glove and were both sturdy and comfortable. They gave her confidence.

She tied her wet clothes into a plastic bag and stuffed them into the duffel. Her hair was still wet, but she'd combed it out. She slung the bulky black bag over her shoulder, jazzed at the prospect of seeing Troy, even knowing her buzz of arousal was a seriously dangerous state.

She exited through the open doorway, finding Vegas standing guard.

"I hope that wasn't too inconvenient," she said as they walked side by side down the hall.

"I didn't mind," he answered.

He looked as though he didn't. And it helped. Vegas seemed both immensely capable and down-to-earth.

"I meant for everyone else," she told him. "It's hard to be one of the guys when you have to lock them out of their own showers."

"I doubt anyone had a shower emergency in the past fifteen minutes."

"You know what I mean."

"I do," he said.

He pressed the button to call the elevator.

"You did good out there," he told her.

"I failed miserably." She hadn't expected to magically pass, but she had hoped to improve her result more than she'd managed.

"You've got grit, Mila. They'll be impressed by that."

"Troy?" she couldn't help but ask.

"Troy doesn't want to be impressed. He's looking for reasons not to be impressed. But you already know that."

"I don't know what to do," she admitted. "It's…" She wanted to say complicated. She wanted to say impossible. But she didn't want to admit the depths of her discouragement to Troy's partner, of all people. "I really don't know what to do."

"If you sleep with him, you'll never be one of the guys."

Mila gaped at Vegas's blunt words.

The elevator door slid open, but she didn't move.

He touched her arm and guided her inside, coming with her. "If you don't sleep with him, both of you will go stark raving mad."

She felt her face heat with embarrassment. "What did he tell you?"

"Nothing. I have eyes. And I'm paid to be observant. And I saw the expression on your face that day at the shooting range. You turned away from Troy, but you were looking at the camera."

She could only imagine what she had revealed to a man like Vegas. "Are people gossiping?"

The elevator rose.

"Maybe," said Vegas. "Though not to me. They're more interested in seeing if you wimp out. And they want to see if Troy cracks on his no-women rule."

"I guess they all know about that?"

"They all know about that."

The number panel flashed past floor five.

"What about a different job?" Vegas asked. "Somewhere other than Pinion."

"Settle for second best?" She shook her head. "That's not in my makeup." And it wasn't in her family's makeup. A job at Pinion might be challenging. But it was what she wanted, and it's what she'd go after.

"You'll really try again?" Vegas asked.

She assumed he meant the obstacle course. "In a couple of days."

"Stay lower in the mud crawl. Use your core strength and save your arms. And don't do the whole course again for practice. Work on the technical parts, the low walls, the logs and the ropes. Don't waste your energy with bad technique."

The elevator came to a halt on nine.

She didn't know what to say. She was exhausted, sore and stupidly close to tears.

She swallowed. "Thank you."

"I'm just treating you like one of the guys."

"That's all I want."

"I know."

The door slid open.

"Don't sleep with him, Mila."

"I won't." She stepped into the hallway, vowing to take that advice.

Vegas gave a sharp nod as the door slid shut.

Her stomach danced with nerves as she made her way to Troy's front door. She knocked once, and he answered almost immediately.

When he didn't say anything, her heart began to thud deeply in her chest. His stance was tense, his gaze penetrating, and his knuckles were white where he gripped the door. Her first thought was that she was about to be fired.

"Uh..." she started haltingly. "You wanted to talk about Kassidy?"

He blinked, as if her words weren't making sense. Then his hand shifted on the door. "Kassidy, right."

"Should I come back later?" She'd like to come back later. She'd rather come back later. Whatever Troy was thinking, she didn't want him to say it out loud.

But he stepped back. "No. Come in."

"Is Kassidy up?"

Company would be a good idea. Would he fire her in front of his sister? Hopefully, Kassidy would take Mila's side.

"You have your laptop?" he asked.

"I do." She wondered where this was leading.

Was he going to suggest she update her résumé? Maybe he'd offer her a letter of reference. Should she take it? Should she beg him to reconsider? Should she slam out of here in righteous anger?

She pictured herself marching out the door. Then she pictured herself begging him to keep her. Then, unfortunately, the image turned to him kissing her, holding her, reassuring her that—

That what? That they'd be good in bed together.

"Let's do it in my office," he said.

Her stomach contracted. "Excuse me?"

He looked annoyed as he shut the door. "Bring your laptop to my office. I want to run through your analysis."

"On Kassidy?" she confirmed, still feeling as though she was changing gears.

"Of course on Kassidy. What is wrong with you?"

"Nothing."

"Did you hit your head out there?"

"I did not hit my head." She started for the office. "I bruised just about everything else," she muttered as she walked.

She wanted to blame him for that. She did blame him for that. The obstacle course was impossible. It was going to kill someone. Probably her.

She entered the room and plunked her duffel bag down on the floor.

"You okay?" he asked, his voice unexpectedly close and unexpectedly even.

She turned.

"Are you hurt?" he asked, scanning her face.

"I'm fine."

"Any falls this time?"

She shook her head. "Just the usual scrapes and bruises."

"You made it farther."

The statement took her by surprise. "You saw me?"

"Only on the monitor."

Had he watched her struggle? Had he judged her performance? Or had he merely happened to glance at the security
monitor as the buzzer went off? There was no way to guess,
and she wasn't going to ask.

"Did you laugh?" she asked instead, hoping to lighten
the mood.

She was feeling better now that it looked as though she
wouldn't be fired today.

"Only the first time, when you…face-planted in the mud."
Then he sobered. "I didn't laugh. I was pulling for you."

"No, you weren't. You're going to hate it when I succeed."

"I think you mean *if* you succeed."

"I think I mean when."

Instead of answering, he touched her collarbone, brushing gently across her skin. "You have a gash."

"It's nothing."

He pulled on the neck of her T-shirt. "It's minor."

"Isn't that what I just said?"

"I needed to see for myself."

"Because you don't trust me?"

"Because I worry about you."

"I'm not made of glass, Troy."

His fingers feathered across her neck. "I wish you were. It
would be so much easier if you were delicate, feminine, and
I could protect you and you wouldn't challenge and protest
every little thing I do."

"Is that what you like?" she dared to ask. "You like help-
less women?"

"I thought I did." He was coming closer. "I thought I
knew exactly the type of woman I liked. And then you came
along. And now I have to question myself. I don't like questioning myself."

She told herself to back away, but she didn't move. "Are
you looking for sympathy?"

"No."

"Good."

"I'm looking for an answer. Yes or no."

"To what?"

He took a step. Then he took her hand. He lined up their lips, canting his head to one side. "Yes or no?"

"No," she managed to whisper, clinging to good sense.

"You sure?"

"No." She wasn't sure at all.

He brushed his lips lightly against hers, starting a trail of desire that warmed her brain.

He paused.

She waited, thinking of his kiss, desperate for his kiss.

"Yes or no?" he repeated.

She groaned in surrender. Her hands went to his waist, and she crossed the miniscule space between them, pressing her lips to his in a hungry kiss.

Troy immediately wrapped her in his arms, pulling her tight, holding her flush against him.

It felt good. It felt so, *so* good. She gave in to the sensations, running her hands along his arms, up to his shoulders, feeling the strength and mass of his muscles. He shouldn't feel so overwhelmingly sexy. Sure, he was fit, and he was buff, but he was just a man. Why couldn't she resist him?

She reached for his buttons, kissing him deeply while her fingers worked his shirt. She separated the fabric, touching his skin, feeling its heat, the play of his muscles, the ridge of a scar, then another and another.

She broke the kiss, gazing down. She kissed the white line that crossed his left ribs.

He gasped, and his hand tunneled into her hair.

The sound of the door swinging shut beside them should have given her pause. But she was beyond caring. She tugged off her T-shirt, then stripped off her bra, putting them skin to skin and tipping her chin for his kiss.

He rumbled her name, bringing his lips back to hers. His hands stroked her bare back. He gathered her close, flattening her against him, the heat and friction building.

He turned them both, lifting her to perch her on the edge of his desk. She widened her thighs so he fit between. She looped her arms around his neck, steadying herself, letting her nipples rub against his chest, the tingles from the contact shooting spikes of desire through her stomach and lower.

He kissed her neck, moving to her breasts, drawing her nipple into his hot mouth.

She grasped the lip of the desk, holding tight as her head tipped back. A moan escaped from her lips. Heat suffused her body. Passion ramped up, blocking out sight and sound as her world contracted to Troy.

She felt him pop the button on her jeans, draw down the zipper. She kicked her boots free, and her jeans came off, followed by her panties.

She reached out to him, getting rid of his pants, desperate to bring them together. His palms cupped her rear, lifting her up, pulling her to him, hot and hard.

She curled to his body, kissing his chest, tasting the salt of his skin, inhaling his musk while his rhythm drew her upward into a spiral of pleasure. He drove her higher, and she panted his name over and over.

He took her mouth, his kisses hot and deep, his tongue tangling with hers, while his hands kneaded her flesh and he thrust and withdrew.

The world seemed to pause and hover at the edge of paradise.

"So good," he groaned, his body turning to heated iron. "Mila. Oh, Mila." His hug tightened, his arms like bands of steel holding her safe.

"Faster," she begged him, feeling the crescendo tingle its way through her limbs. "Please."

"Yes," he growled, increasing his speed. "Yes."

Her hands tightened on his shoulders, struggling for an anchor as passion threatened to pull her apart.

"Troy," she cried out as her body imploded.

His body shuddered in return.

Then his kisses grew gentle. He stroked her hair. He cradled her body, taking her weight against himself.

Reality returned to her.

She'd had sex with Troy.

This was bad. It was very, very bad.

They were naked. And he was still inside her. And heaven help her, it still felt fantastic.

"Oh, no," she moaned. "Oh, no."

He tensed.

She drew back. "We didn't just do that."

He glanced down to where their bodies were joined. "We didn't?"

"No." She slipped free, wiggling back on the desk. "It was an accident. We didn't think it through." Her brain was desperately scrambling for an out. "It's not like we had dinner and wine, candles and lingerie, a big bed and a night together."

"That was an option?" he asked.

She smacked him on the shoulder. "Work with me here. This *can't* have happened." She hopped off the desk, searching for her clothes. "You're my boss. I'm one of the guys."

She found her bra and her T-shirt. She glanced over her shoulder to find him perusing her backside. "Stop!"

"Mila, you've never been one of the guys."

"You know what I mean." She grabbed her panties from the floor and pulled them on, covering up.

She put on her bra and covered it up with her T-shirt. There, that felt better. Better still, she was climbing into her jeans.

Troy quickly got dressed, too, running spread fingers through his short hair, while Mila tightened the laces on her boots.

She came to her feet to face him. "This never happened."

He looked more amused than upset. "You're rewriting history?"

"It can't impact anything we do or anything we think.

We're going to review my notes on Kassidy and discuss her case on its merits. We're putting everything else out of our minds, and we are never, ever telling a soul."

"You mean, we're never telling anyone what didn't happen?"

It took her a second to wrap her head around his statement. "Yes. Exactly. It's like we both had the same fantasy, but it wasn't real."

He looked skeptical, and she didn't exactly buy into it herself. But it was her only hope.

Sitting beside and slightly behind Mila at his office desk, Troy watched her scroll through her analysis of Kassidy's last few performances. It was a struggle to understand the words. He was mostly listening to the sound of her voice, inhaling the wintergreen scent of her hair, and stopping himself from brushing the bare skin of her arm.

"So Edison checked the cell tower traffic for those exact times," she said. "I like Edison."

That got Troy's attention. "What do you mean you like Edison?"

"I mean he's a big help. So is Vegas. So is Charlie."

Troy hated the surge of jealousy that rose in his gut. "What have you been doing with Charlie?"

"I work well with your staff, Troy. We cooperate. I'm a team player. You should think about that."

"I am thinking about that." He hated picturing Mila talking, laughing, doing anything with members of his staff.

"They originated from the same burner phone."

"What? Who?"

She turned her head. "What's the matter with you?"

"Nothing." Unless you counted the fact that his brain was still reeling from having made love to her.

Yes, he'd made love to Mila. And it had been off-the-charts fantastic. He wanted to do it again. It was all he could do not to sit forward and wrap his arms around her. She was in fantastic shape, but also soft in all the right places. She smelled like paradise, and she tasted sweeter than fifty-year-old brandy. And she had about as much of a kick.

He couldn't help but smile in satisfaction.

She gave him a look of disgust. "Like I said, the guy in the blazer. He was back on Saturday night. He was texting, and I wrote down the times." She focused on the screen again, her voice going no-nonsense. "I jotted down as many as I could, then I correlated them to the information from the cell tower. I got a burner number. But the interesting thing is that some of the times coincided with posts to Kassidy from MeMy-Heart and BluebellNighthawk. It's one person."

"Lots of people have two accounts."

As far as Troy was concerned, all Mila had identified was a fan. Sure, she'd matched a face with two account names and a burner phone. But that didn't mean the guy wasn't a perfectly ordinary fan.

"He drives a black SUV," she said.

"Did you get the plate number?" Now *that* would be useful.

"He was too far away."

"So we have nothing."

"We don't have nothing. This is the guy who mentioned Drake. Charlie's coming with us on Thursday. He'll watch for the SUV. I'll watch Kassidy, and Edison will monitor the electronic traffic."

"Vegas is coordinating?"

Her shoulders tensed, and her voice went cold. "You can't even fake it, can you?"

He didn't know what she was trying to say, but he was sure he didn't like it. "I don't fake anything."

"Yes, Vegas knows about the plan. But he's not coordinating. This is my operation, Troy. I'm leading the investigation. I'm creating the strategy."

"As long as Vegas is there for quality control."

She pivoted the swivel chair. "You won't give me a chance, will you? You won't give me a single break."

A break? She wanted a break, after all those speeches insisting she be treated like one of the guys? Now she sat there with her big green eyes, her rosy cheeks, that soft skin and kissable mouth, wanting special treatment?

His voice came out harsher than he'd intended. "What kind of a break would you like, sweetheart?"

Her expression went hard. "Go to hell." She jumped to her feet.

He shot up with her, grasping her arm. "What makes you think I'm not already there?"

While he glared at her, his lungs labored, and sweat broke out on his brow. It didn't matter that they'd made love half an hour before, he was desperate to do it again.

"You think you can hold me?" she asked.

He wanted to hold her. That much he knew.

She unexpectedly slammed her fist into his solar plexus. "I can take care of myself."

The power behind her fist shocked him, and he staggered back.

She braced herself, stood ready, as if she thought he was going to hit her back.

He held up his palms to show her he had no intention of retaliating. He wouldn't hit her. He'd never hit her.

Her eyes narrowed, and her face screwed up in obvious disappointment. "No," she cried and took a menacing step forward.

"I am not going to fight you," he told her.

"Defend yourself."

"Stop."

She made a fist, and he grabbed and held her hand. But she was quick, she'd obviously anticipated his move, and she pivoted, putting him off balance.

"Stop," he shouted.

He wrapped his arms around her from behind, clamping down while she wiggled to get free.

The door suddenly swung open, and Kassidy appeared.

"Troy!" She gaped at her brother in obvious horror.

He immediately released Mila.

"What are you doing?"

"She attacked me."

Kassidy headed across the room. "What did you do to her?" She put a comforting arm around Mila's shoulders.

He was disgusted. Talk about having it both ways.

"I started it," said Mila.

"Too bad," said Kassidy, still glaring at him. "He's the man."

"No, he's *not* the man." Then Mila seemed to realize how that sounded. "I mean, he *is* a man. But we're both…"

Troy couldn't help himself. "Men?"

She glared at him. "Equals."

"He's got a hundred pounds on you," said Kassidy.

"Almost," Troy agreed.

"I'm faster," said Mila clamping her jaw.

"No, you're not," he countered.

"What are you two fighting about?" Kassidy asked.

Mila blinked, looking momentarily confused.

He couldn't remember, either.

"He's stubborn," said Mila.

"She's opinionated," he said.

"We were talking about your fans," she added.

"Yeah. Your fans. And your gigs. And your security."

"I have a plan." Mila shrugged. "And he's trying to give Vegas the credit."

"I am not." That wasn't remotely close to what he'd told her. "If you were a man," he said to Mila. *"If* you *were,* in fact, a man, I'd have Vegas sticking to you like glue."

She folded her arms across her chest. "Because I'm incompetent?"

"Will you two stop shouting?" Kassidy broke in.

Then he heard it. Drake was crying in the bedroom.

"Thanks a lot," said Kassidy. "I was hoping to get a cup of coffee first."

Troy experienced an unexpected and unwanted shot of guilt. It was his apartment, for goodness' sake. He wasn't allowed to raise his voice in his own apartment?

"I'll get him." Even as he made the offer, he wondered why he was doing it.

Maybe just to get away. Maybe to put some distance between him and Mila. He sure needed it.

For a while there, he'd thought making love to her would get things out of his system. He thought that if he stopped wondering about it, stopped speculating on what it would be like, stopped imagining her naked, he could stop obsessing over her.

That was a mistake. Making love to her was better than he could have imagined. She was more beautiful than he'd ever dreamed. The obsession wasn't gone. It was worse now than ever.

He paced his way across the living room, finding Drake in the dim bedroom, up on his hands and knees in his crib bawling his eyes out.

Troy gently lifted the baby, cradling him against his chest, stroking his hair.

"Poor thing," he crooned. "Who wants to wake up all alone in the dark?"

He laid the baby down on top of the dresser, which was the makeshift changing table. He'd gotten pretty fast at changing a diaper. Though Drake fussed, it was over quickly, and he was back in Troy's arms.

Troy patted Drake's back as he left the bedroom, heading for the kitchen and a bottle of formula.

"Who wants to wake up all alone in the dark?" he repeated in a soothing undertone, even as he pictured his own empty bed. "I wish I could tell you it gets better, little guy. But life is full of long, long, lonely nights."

Nine

Mila was working with two new pieces of information from last night's performance, and Vegas had assigned her a desk in the bullpen. Sitting next to Charlie, an irreverent, handsome twenty-something and the newest employee of Pinion, she was beginning to feel more like a member of the team.

Charlie didn't seem to have Troy's bias against women. He'd worked the street outside the club last night, photographing all of the black SUVs in the vicinity. Now he was working through facial recognition databases with the best picture she'd taken of the blazer guy. If they could get a name, they might match it to a license plate.

The man had been right up front by the stage this time. She'd been tempted to talk to him, but the last thing she wanted to do was tip her hand. She'd checked with the bartender, but the man hadn't bought a drink. Too bad—a credit card receipt or a glass with fingerprints would have been nice.

At the same time, she didn't want to fixate on him. She hadn't seen him send any messages last night, yet Kassidy had received seven from both MeMyHeart and Bluebell-Nighthawk.

It could still be someone else.

She was reviewing another long list of messages when something caught her eye.

"Hang on," she said to Charlie.

There were three other agents working in the room, creating a backdrop of telephone conversations, newsfeeds and the hum of equipment.

"What is it?" he asked, looking up from his monitor.

"It's on the MeMyHeart account. He says the usual stuff—she's beautiful, talented, looks good in pink. He does seem to have a thing for pink. But get this: 'when we're reunited, all together again, and you are my own.'"

"Creep level of about four," said Charlie.

"I'd give it a five. But here's the thing, the words *all together again*. Does that sound like more than two? Together again would be two. All together is more."

"Maybe."

"Maybe three?" She sorted her way through possibilities.

"Could be," said Charlie.

"Drake makes three."

Charlie looked up at her.

Mila quickly went back to her computer and scrolled through MeMyHeart's previous posts.

He'd mentioned Drake. He'd mentioned the baby more than once. Could he have meant the three of them all together? He'd also used the word *again*. Had the three of them somehow been together in the past?

A shiver ran up her spine. Could blazer guy have something to do with Drake? Were they coming at this backward? Could Drake possibly be the conduit to Kassidy?

She brought up blazer guy's picture and hit print. She had to show it to Kassidy.

"I'm going upstairs," she told Charlie.

"You got something?"

"Just a hunch. I won't be long."

"Anything I can do?"

She went for the printer. "Find me a name for blazer guy. That'll make my day."

"Working on it."

She paused with the printed picture in her hand. "Thanks, Charlie."

He looked puzzled. "Just doing my job."

"I mean, thanks for treating me like one of the guys."

He gave a small smile. "You are one of the guys."

The words warmed her heart.

He went back to his work. "I'll call you if anything comes through."

"Thanks."

She was on the third floor, and she took the stairs to nine, knocking on Troy's apartment door.

While she waited, she realized that it could be Troy who opened the door. It was almost noon, and he often had lunch in the apartment. She hadn't seen him since their disastrous lovemaking. She hoped she wasn't about to see him now.

What would she do? What would she say? More importantly, what would he do, and what would he say? Would he ignore it as she'd asked? Would he allude to it? Would he make a move?

If he made a move, she'd absolutely call him on it and tell him in no uncertain terms to keep his hands to himself. She wasn't about to become the boss's plaything.

As she thought about his hands—what they'd done to her, what they could do to her—her skin heated up and a gleam of desire began in her core. The man had magic hands, magic lips, magic—

The doorknob rattled, and she braced herself.

But it was Kassidy who opened the door.

Mila told herself she was relieved.

"Hey, Mila." Kassidy was jiggling Drake in her arms.

The baby grinned when he saw Kassidy, holding out his arms and leaning toward her.

"Oh, sure," Kassidy chided with a smile. "Go to Auntie Mila. Never mind that I'm the one who feeds, changes and rocks you to sleep."

Mila lifted Drake, settling him against her hip while he cooed and grabbed at the leather bag strap on her shoulder.

"Got a minute?" she asked Kassidy.

"You bet. Want a coffee? Gabby's making pancakes, breakfast for me, lunch for Drake. Have I told you that I love her? I love, love, *love* her."

Mila laughed. Kassidy had been singing the nanny's praises ever since she was hired. "You may have mentioned it once or twice. Drake eats pancakes?"

"Mostly he plays with them. But a little bit gets ingested."

"Yes to the coffee. No thanks on the pancakes."

Kassidy led the way to the kitchen. "What do you want to talk about?"

Mila extracted the picture of blazer guy from her shoulder bag. "Does this man look familiar?"

Kassidy accepted the picture.

"Hi, Mila," Gabby greeted from where she stood over a frying pan, flipper in hand.

She was in her early twenties, good-humored, down-to-earth. She had a diploma in early childhood education and had just become engaged to a chiropractor. She was willing to work flexible hours, and Drake adored her.

"Was that at the performance last night?" asked Kassidy.

Mila had been careful to keep Kassidy from getting unduly worried or upset. So she hadn't shared a lot of information with her.

"I saw him texting a few times that coincided with messages you received. It's a bit of a long shot, but if there's anything you can tell me about him?"

"Vaguely familiar," said Kassidy, squinting at the picture. "If he's been up front at the stage before, I probably remember him from that."

Kassidy handed the picture back and reached for Drake. "Come to Kassidy, sweetheart. Are you hungry?"

Gabby handed Mila a cup of coffee.

Mila inhaled the aroma. "Thanks." She took a drink.

Kassidy sat Drake in his high chair, fastening a clean bib around his neck.

"One more question," said Mila. It was even more of a long shot, but she wanted to be completely thorough on the Drake angle.

"Sure," said Kassidy.

"Did you know Drake's father?"

Kassidy froze. The color drained from her face.

"Kassidy?"

"No," Kassidy said brightly, giving Drake's shoulders a squeeze and smoothing his fine hair.

"Are you sure?"

"Of course I'm sure."

"You faltered there."

Kassidy looked up. "It was a rough time. The guy was a one-night stand. And then Drake's mom got sick. The whole thing was very upsetting."

"I'm sorry," said Mila, but her brain was ticking about a hundred miles an hour.

There was something about Drake's father, something that had Kassidy worried. It was an outlandish theory. But could the stalker be Drake's father? Could blazer guy be Drake's father?

Mila finished her coffee and headed back to the bullpen.

Charlie was gone, but Troy was staring at her monitor.

Her chest tightened at the sight of him. Her pulse jumped and butterflies formed in her stomach.

Troy looked up, his expression smooth and professional. She schooled her own.

"This is from last night?" he asked.

She moved to where she could see the screen. "Yes. That's the blazer guy I said I thought was suspicious."

"There's something…" said Troy.

"What is it?"

"He looks familiar."

"You know him?"

That was significant.

"I can't place him." Troy picked up the phone and dialed. "Take a look at the picture up on Mila's computer."

"Who's that?" she asked.

"Vegas," Troy told her. "Anything?" Troy said into the phone. Then he waited for a moment. "I've come across him somewhere before. Why can't I remember? It's definitely been a few years."

Another moment passed.

"Are you sure?" Troy asked Vegas. "Yeah. This might be something completely different. I'll be right there." He hung up the phone.

"What?" asked Mila.

"I know that guy. This might have nothing to do with Kassidy. It could be about me."

Mila wrapped her head around the theory. It was possible. The same way the Drake link was possible. She hated having so many tenuous threads.

"Kassidy might have crazy fans." Troy rose and started for the door. "But I've ticked off some very dangerous people over the years."

Mila followed, coming at Troy's theory from as many angles as she could muster. "Why target her?"

"To get to me."

"There are easier ways to get to you."

"Not really. I'm cautious. I'm prepared. I'm always armed."

"I don't mean get to you as in harm you. I mean upset you."

"I'm pretty upset."

They made their way down the hall to Vegas and Troy's office.

"It started when she was in New Jersey."

"So?"

"So, the two of you were estranged. You said yourself, you only saw her once a year."

"She's still my half sister. I've always stepped up when she needed it." He marched through the office doorway. "She's in my building. She's in my apartment." He spoke to Vegas. "We need to do a full sweep."

Mila looked for flaws. The notes to Kassidy were personal. The writer seemed to be obsessing about her and Drake, not about Troy.

"Where does Drake fit in?" Mila asked.

"He's incidental."

"He's mentioned in the posts. You're not."

"So what? He's part of her life, part of my life. This is a whole lot bigger than a rabid fan."

Vegas was on his cell, heading for the door.

"Don't let Kassidy out of your sight," Troy called to him.

"I'll go," said Mila.

"I want Vegas."

"I can handle it," said Mila, moving to follow.

But Troy grasped her arm to stop her. "This is above your pay grade."

"Excuse me?" She tried to shake him off, but his grip was tight.

"I'm not leaving this to you. You're inexperienced, you're temporary, you're—"

"Female?"

"I didn't say that."

"You didn't have to. You've said it a thousand times."

"This isn't about you being a woman."

"This is *all* about me being a woman. It's another of your knee-jerk reactions."

He glared at her in obvious anger.

"This might be about you," she allowed. "But it could still be about Kassidy and Drake. It could even be all about Drake."

"Drake?"

"Yes."

"Based on what? Evidence? Facts? Because I definitely recognize the guy. That means he's somewhere in my past."

"You don't remember where. It could be anywhere. Don't ignore everything else."

Troy's jaw tightened.

"There's a very good chance you're wrong," said Mila.

They stared at each other, their gazes locked. Emotions raced through her—frustration, annoyance, anxiety, exasperation. At least it wasn't sexual attraction. She had that going for her.

"Are you *looking* to get fired?" he ground out.

She kept her stare level and steady. "I was never hired."

"Kassidy likes you. That's the only thing you have going for you. You can stay and follow my orders, or you can leave, right now."

Mila wanted to leave. She'd take great emotional satisfaction from turning on her heel and walking away.

But that wouldn't help Kassidy. And it wouldn't help Drake. They were innocent in all of this. If Troy was wrong, if he fixated on the wrong problem, the two of them could be in real danger.

It was better to stay and do what she could, everything she could, even if it meant going behind Troy's back, following her own leads and risking his wrath.

Later in the week, Vegas sat in a leather armchair in Troy's living room. He had a computer printout in his hand, one ankle resting on the opposite knee. "I warned her not to sleep with you."

Troy stared back, anger warring with disbelief.

"Maybe I should have told *you* not to sleep with *her*."

"She *told* you that?" Troy was shocked to think Mila might have confided in Vegas.

"She didn't have to tell me a thing."

"Then you're guessing."

"Your judgment is clouded."

Troy's gaze flicked to the closed door of Kassidy's room. Mila was with her in there. She'd chosen to stay, and she'd agreed to take direction from Troy.

"My judgment is fine," he said.

"Why did you do it?"

Troy decided to brazen it out, force Vegas to put his cards on the table, if he had any cards. "What makes you think I did?"

"You might as well have worn a neon sign Sunday night. Jovial, relaxed, satiated. Too bad it didn't last."

Troy had no interest in this conversation, but he wasn't going to lie, either. "It was a mistake. It's over and done. It has no bearing on this."

"You don't want her to get hurt."

Troy felt the jab directly in the center of his chest. "I don't want anybody to get hurt."

"Especially not her."

"Can we end this conversation?"

Vegas shifted his leg and leaned forward. "Problem you've got is, it wasn't about sex."

Troy sat up straight. "I'm serious. This conversation is *done*."

"You have feelings for her."

"What do I have to do to shut you up?"

"You're protecting her."

"I'm *protecting* Kassidy."

"You're protecting Mila. It was bad enough when she was just another woman, just another Gabriela—"

"Shut up." Troy rose to his feet, his stomach twisting into a knot.

Mila wasn't Gabriela. But she was a woman. And Troy had learned from Gabriela. He *had* to have learned from Gabriela. Otherwise, Gabriela had died in vain.

Vegas set down his report and stood more slowly. "She's an asset."

"She's a *person*."

"So am I. So are you. So are Edison and Charlie."

Troy glared at him. "She's not like Edison and Charlie."

"Trust her," said Vegas. "You like her. You want her. I know you admire her. Now you've got to trust her."

"I *won't* kill her."

"This isn't about you."

"You're right. It's about her, and what's best for her. And what we do, who we are, is not best for her."

"That's not for you to decide."

"Yes, it is."

It was. Troy could decide to hire her, or he could decide to let her go. Letting her go was safe. Hiring her was fraught with risk.

Kassidy's bedroom door opened, and Mila appeared.

Troy watched as she approached, unable to look away, his emotions hovering at the surface. She was wearing her usual cargo pants, tan colored today. They were topped with an olive-green T-shirt that stretched across her breasts, covering her shoulders in cap sleeves. Her hair was braided, her makeup nonexistent, and her worn leather boots were as serviceable as footwear could be.

She was drop-dead gorgeous.

He had to stop himself from going to her.

"We need to leave for the club in about fifteen minutes," she told them.

"I'm coming," said Troy.

She gave a nod, as if she'd expected the decision.

"I'll take backstage tonight," Troy stated. "Vegas will be at the door, and Charlie will be outside."

"What about me?"

He wanted to tell her to stay here, to lie low with Drake and the nanny. As the thought flashed through his mind, he realized Vegas was at least partially right. Troy did want to keep Mila safe.

His feelings for her weren't just about sex, and they weren't just professional. He liked her far too much, and he wanted to protect her.

"I'll mix with the crowd," she spoke into his silence. Then she looked down at her outfit. "But I'm not going to blend in this."

"Don't spook the guy," said Troy.

She gave him a look of reproach. "I won't."

"I want to see him in action, walking, talking." It was the best plan he'd come up with. "Maybe that'll jog my memory."

"I'll go put on something sexy."

Troy's throat went suddenly dry.

"I'm sure Kassidy has an outfit I can borrow. Maybe blazer guy will buy me a drink."

"No." Troy didn't want Mila that close to the guy.

She frowned. "If he uses his credit card, we get his name. If I'm going to have the downsides of being a woman, I might as well have the upsides as well."

"No," Troy repeated.

"It's not a bad plan," said Vegas.

"Stay out of this."

"Have I recently resigned as your partner?" asked Vegas. "Because I used to have a say in operations."

"It's a dangerous plan."

"It's a *drink*," said Mila. "And Vegas will be right there. Not to mention you. Come on, Troy. Get a grip."

"We don't know who this guy is."

Even as he said the words, Troy realized he was outdone. Vegas had an equal say in company operations. Troy couldn't veto him. Besides, they were right. It was a reasonable plan. The danger was minimal. He didn't know what was wrong with him.

"That would be the point," said Mila, moving closer. "I can clean up. I can look like a girl. I could attract a guy's attention."

Troy opened his mouth, about to tell her she'd knock any guy with a pulse off his feet. He caught Vegas's knowing smirk in his peripheral vision.

"Okay," he said instead.

The answer seemed to take her by surprise. But she quickly recovered. "Give me ten minutes." She headed back to Kassidy's room.

Mila felt conspicuous dressed in Kassidy's short kilt skirt. It was deep blue and green tones, pleated and flirty, barely falling to her midthighs. She'd paired it with a cropped black angora sweater, the sleeves pushed up above her elbows.

Kassidy had layered on some dramatic makeup while

Mila had brushed out her hair. It was wavy now and looked slightly disheveled from the earlier French braid. She'd never attempted heels this high, but judging by the lingering looks coming her way, the outfit was working.

She hadn't spotted the blazer guy yet. But she'd had three offers of drinks from other men. Through her discreet earpiece, Vegas surprised her with his sense of humor in response to the pickup lines. Troy seemed less than amused, warning her away from the men. As if she was about to get swept off her feet by: "Hey, girl. This is your lucky day."

She camouflaged her lips with her hand. "I've done this before, Troy."

"Been picked up in bars?"

Vegas jumped in. "She means been hit on in bars."

Charlie coughed out a laugh before he obviously switched off his mic.

"That's what I meant," she confirmed.

"You go into bars alone?" asked Troy.

"Sure."

"Dressed like *that*?"

"It doesn't matter what I'm wearing."

"Guys are easy," said Vegas.

"Guys are hound dogs," said Troy.

"Nice to hear one of you admit it," said Mila.

"Your two o'clock," said Vegas, his tone turning serious.

She glanced toward the front door, confirming blazer guy's location before letting her gaze move onward, pretending to scan for the restroom.

"That's him," she said. "How long until Kassidy comes out?"

"Ten minutes," said Troy.

Mila watched while the blazer guy made his way to the bar. He spoke to the bartender, who poured him an ice water.

"Going in," she muttered.

"Go get 'im," said Charlie.

"Enough commentary," said Troy, his tone clipped.

Mila wanted to tell him to lighten up, but she was pretty sure that would only make matters worse.

She sidled her way up to the bar, setting down her clutch purse and leaning forward. She didn't have a lot of cleavage, but by strategically placing her arms and letting the V neck of the sweater gape, she made the most of what she had.

The bartender was there in a heartbeat. Unfortunately, blazer guy barely glanced her way.

"Get you something?" asked the bartender.

"Neapolitan martini."

"Vodka?"

"Yes."

"Preference on the brand?"

"Give me your best."

"You got it." The man smiled as he withdrew.

Mila turned her attention to the blazer guy, staring openly at his profile, waiting for him to turn her way.

He slanted her a glance but didn't turn, instead taking a sip of his ice water.

She slipped onto the bar stool, watching the bartender work and toying with a cardboard coaster.

"Eight minutes," said Troy.

"I don't think that's helpful," said Vegas.

"Ask him about his jacket," offered Charlie. "The designer or whatever."

Mila inwardly rolled her eyes. She moved her elbow and knocked her purse to the ground. It landed with a clatter, the contents spilling out.

That got his attention.

"My phone," she cried, clambering down, pretending to stumble and leaning into him.

He quickly grasped her arms, steadying her.

"I'm so sorry," she gasped. "It's these heels."

Predictably, he looked down to see the four-inch strappy black shoes, replete with winking rhinestones.

"Could you?" she asked prettily, gesturing to the mess.

BARBARA DUNLOP   139

He glanced to the stage, hesitating before answering. "Sure."

She put a hand on his arm. "Thank you *so* much."

Then she bent down with him, exploiting her cleavage.

"Nice," said Vegas.

"Is that how women do it?" asked Charlie.

"Careful," said Troy.

Mila wanted to ask why she had to be careful. They were in a crowded bar, and she had three bodyguards. It wasn't as though the guy could spike her drink.

He gathered up her lipstick, cell phone, wallet and keys, then rose and handed her the purse.

"Thank you," she repeated, giving him an overly encouraging smile. "I'm Sandy." She held out her hand.

Again, he hesitated.

"Jack," he told her, accepting the handshake.

"Lie," said Charlie.

Jack's hand was soft, almost limp. Not a tradesman, she concluded. His skin was pale, so he didn't work outside. And his shoulders and arms seemed slim. She doubted he had a physical job at all. Maybe he was an accountant or an office manager.

"Three minutes," said Troy.

The bartender put the drink down in front of her and she quickly took a swallow, then another and another.

"That's commitment," said Vegas.

"This is fantastic," she enthused.

The bartender gave her a smile.

"I wouldn't mind another," she mused, finishing the glass.

Jack didn't pick up on the hint.

Unfortunately, the bartender was quicker on the draw. "Coming up."

Mila took another tactic, gesturing toward a poster of Kassidy. "I've heard she's a good singer."

Something came into "Jack's" eyes—possessiveness, defensiveness and caution. This had to be their guy.

"Have you heard her before?" Mila asked.

"A couple of times." His tone was flat.

"You like her?"

His glare told Mila he would prefer she shut up and go away.

"Made of frickin' stone," Charlie muttered.

"Quiet," Troy ordered. "One minute."

The bartender set the fresh drink down in front of her. He looked to Jack. Clearly, he was picking up on the vibes she was sending out.

But Jack ignored him.

"On the house," the bartender told her.

"Thanks." But she extracted a twenty from her purse and pushed it toward him.

"I'm coming over to pay for the drink myself," said Vegas on a note of disgust.

The bartender took the bill. He looked to Jack and gave a pitying shake of his head.

The lights came up on the stage, and the opening bars of Kassidy's first song rang through the room. Jack immediately vacated his bar stool and made his way forward.

"Got him," said Vegas.

"Good effort, Mila," said Charlie.

"Coming up on stage left," said Vegas.

"Got him," said Troy.

Mila sighed her defeat and took a sip of the new drink.

"Dumb as a bag of hammers," said the bartender.

Mila gave a shrug. "Maybe he's got a girlfriend. Have you seen him in here before?"

"Once that I remember," said the bartender. "Three weeks ago. Same singer."

"Yeah?" Mila turned her attention.

"He wasn't with a girl that time."

"Did he stick to ice water?"

"Cheap," said the bartender.

"My take was that he lied about his name." Mila let the statement hang.

"You ask, and I'll give you *my* name, my address and phone number, and the keys to my apartment." The grin and waggle of his eyebrows turned the statement into a joke.

"You need help?" asked Troy.

"She's fine," said Vegas. "Focus on Kassidy."

Yes, focus on Kassidy. What was Troy's problem?

"You ever get that guy's name?" Mila decided to come right out with it.

"Don't tell me you're still interested." The bartender sounded incredulous.

"Only curious," said Mila. She took another sip of the drink. "Maybe it's my ego. I'd like to know what went wrong."

"What went wrong is that he's a prize idiot. That's what went wrong."

"Gotta agree with that," said Charlie.

"Back off," said Troy, sounding genuinely ticked off. "Jack's at the edge of the stage. He's texting."

Mila went for her phone. Edison had set it up so that she could intercept Kassidy's messages.

"Six, six seven," said the bartender.

"Cute," said Mila.

She brought up Kassidy's messages. Sure enough, there was a new one from MeMyHeart.

The bartender moved to serve another customer.

"New message, MeMyHeart," Mila said in an undertone.

"Can you read it?" asked Edison from the control room back at Pinion.

The bartender returned. "You need another drink?"

"No, thanks. This is fine." She decided to give it one final try. "So that Jack guy, he never paid for anything with a credit card?"

The bartender's eyes narrowed, suspicion coming into his expression. "You a cop?"

"Not a cop." She searched for a cover story. "I have a sister," she said, then took a drink to buy herself some time. "That guy, well, he lied to her, treated her like crap."

"You're looking for payback?"

"I am."

The bartender shook his head. "Wish I could help you. Believe me, if I could rack up some points with you, I would."

Mila couldn't help but smile at his candor. "I'd give you points if you could come up with something. Anything."

"Drank only water. Watched the show. Left alone. That's all I can tell you."

She came to her feet. "Thanks anyway."

"So, no chance I'm getting your number?"

"No chance," said Troy.

"Sorry," said Mila. "But you seem like a good guy."

"Good guy," the bartender mocked. "Always the good guy."

"See you later," she told him as she moved away.

"I won't count on that," he called from behind her.

"Keep right on walking," Troy said in her ear.

Ten

It was impossible for Troy not to see the way men stared at Mila as she crossed the parking lot at the end of the performance. He was surprised by how many fans stayed back to catch Kassidy leaving through the back door, including the guy who'd called himself Jack.

They didn't have a whole lot more information from tonight, except to be positive that Jack was Kassidy's problem fan. He was definitely the guy sending messages as MeMyHeart and BluebellNighthawk.

Troy was also certain he'd seen him before. Vegas didn't recognize him, nor did anyone else on their staff. But Troy couldn't shake the impression this had something to do with him and Pinion. Kassidy was somehow a pawn.

They decided that Charlie would tail Jack while Vegas took Kassidy in his car. Mila would debrief with Troy on the ride back to Pinion. They needed to plan their next move. And she needed to accept that it would be Troy's call, not hers.

She'd done decent foundational work, but real threats were involved. She hadn't accepted that the situation likely centered on Troy, and he wanted to duke it out with her in private. He couldn't let her challenge him in front of his staff.

If he used kid gloves, it undermined his authority. And if he fired her…if he fired her, she'd be gone from his life. And he wasn't ready for that.

She was thirty feet from his vehicle, looking cold without her coat, being stopped by a couple of men. The two guys had obviously been drinking and were leering at her. Why hadn't she covered up with her coat? It was barely fifty degrees. She had to be freezing.

He rocked away from the SUV, intent on sending the two jerks packing. But her glare warned him off. Was that an order? Had the woman just given him a silent order?

Then she was moving again, coming closer, her little skirt

swaying against her smooth, tanned legs, her wavy hair rising and falling with her steps. She was graceful, beautiful, stunningly sexy. He wanted to grab her and kiss her, hold her tight and show every man in this parking lot that she belonged to him.

But she didn't. And he had no right to touch her. And that fact was probably going to kill him before this was all over.

He opened the passenger door. "How are you not freezing?"

She shivered at the suggestion. "My jacket didn't go with the outfit."

"You've been finished with the barfly act for a while now." He couldn't help a glance at the two guys who were still standing in the middle of the parking lot watching her.

He gave them a *back the heck off* glare, holding it until they looked away.

"It's in Vegas's car."

"Why didn't you get it? Or ask me to get it? Or ask Vegas to get it?"

"Are you done?"

His grip tightened on the open door. "Done what?"

"Criticizing me? Coddling me? Whatever it is you're doing. Can we please get in now and start the engine, maybe warm up?"

He swore under his breath and shrugged out of his jacket.

"Oh, no, you don't," she protested, backing away.

He swiftly wrapped his jacket around her, pulling her toward him.

"I'm one of the guys, remember?"

She was way too close to be one of the guys.

He zipped her in as if it were a straitjacket. "Get in."

"Is that an order?"

The jacket was roomy enough that she wiggled her arms into the sleeves, pushing them up to reveal her hands.

"It's an order," he confirmed.

"Yes, sir." She gave a mock salute and turned.

He impulsively patted her on the butt. Then he cringed, bracing himself for instant retaliation.

She froze, but didn't hit him. "Are you suicidal?"

"I may be. Sorry," he added.

"You *can't* do that."

"I know." Then the joke all but leaped out of him. "It's the skirt."

She made an inarticulate moan of protest. "How can you *be* like that?"

"This is why women can't work at Pinion."

She shifted to face him. "Because you'll manhandle them?"

"Because we don't do politically correct."

"Try, Troy. Summon some strength and *try*." She plunked herself down on the passenger seat.

He slammed the door, cussing himself out as he rounded the SUV. What was the matter with him? *Don't touch her.* It was one objective, one rule. How hard could that be?

It was five long minutes before she spoke.

"We need a name," she said.

And he realized she hadn't been sitting there stewing over his behavior.

She popped open her little purse. "We have his fingerprints."

Troy glanced to her lap, and he couldn't help a smile of admiration. "That's why you dropped your purse?"

"That and to get his attention. Seriously, Troy. Is this not a hot outfit?"

"It's a very hot outfit."

He didn't like to recall how hot it was. Because that made him hot. For her. And he didn't dare let his mind go there.

"The man's got a thing for Kassidy. I know you believe this is all about you, but I could have been a block of concrete for all he cared."

"Or he's focused on revenge. Guys like that don't have normal reactions to anything."

"I'm not being conceited," she said.

"Who said you were?"

"It's not that I think I'm super attractive. I get that I'm pretty plain."

Troy would vehemently disagree with that statement.

"But men aren't that picky," she said.

"You're not plain."

She waved away the sentiment. "I have a sister who's a bombshell. Trust me, I know the difference. My point is this Jack guy truly does have an obsession for Kassidy."

"And *my* point is, you are incredibly hot in that outfit tonight. I can't stop picturing it. I can't stop thinking about you. I can't stop *wanting*—"

"Don't." Her voice was so soft, he barely heard it.

He jammed the brakes and swung the vehicle to the side of the road, putting it in Park and angling to face her. "I can't control it."

"You can."

"Can you?"

"Yes."

"You're lying. You said I have a tell. Well, so do you. When you lie, your knees get tight."

"That's not true." But she glanced to her knees.

"For most people, it's in the face. You say it's my left ear, and I believe you. So, tell me, Mila." He turned his head to show the left side of his face. "Am I lying?"

He gave her a moment to focus. And he gave himself a moment to focus. His chest tightened up, and a part of his brain yelled at him to shut up. But he didn't want to shut up. He had to say it out loud.

"I can't stop thinking about you. And it's not just sex."

"No."

"I know you want to be one of the guys. And I wish you could be one of the guys. But it isn't going to happen. I can't keep you, but I can't bring myself to send you away."

"Let me prove myself."

"It doesn't work like that." He'd give anything to banish

the knowledge, the sickening certainty that told him how this all ended.

"Then how does it work? Tell me how it works, and I'll do it."

"You want to know how it works?"

"Yes!"

"You *die*, that's how it works."

"Huh?" Her expression turned to complete confusion.

"Maybe not today. Maybe not tomorrow. But I send you into a situation, and you're overpowered, and it all goes south, and you end up like Gabriela, in a body bag."

"Gabriela?"

"No amount of skill…intellect…or conditioning can prepare you for the guy who's six feet four and can bench-press a compact car."

"Nobody can overpower everybody."

"There's a mathematical odds element."

She seemed to frame her thoughts. "Who's Gabriela?"

"A security agent. A former security agent."

"Did she…?"

"She died."

Mila put a hand on his shoulder. "I'm so sorry."

"It was my fault."

"I'm sure it wasn't."

"You don't know anything about it." He gave into the urge to cover her hand with his.

"I know you." Her gaze was penetrating and honest. "You know what you're doing. You don't take chances. You don't make mistakes."

He squeezed her hand. "Nobody's perfect. I'll mess up again. It's only a matter of time. And I couldn't stand it…" He couldn't stand it if she was on the firing line when he did.

The street was dark. The car was dark. The glow of the dashboard reflected the smooth skin of her cheek. She was so close.

He reached out, stroked the pad of his thumb ever so gently against her cheek.

"Troy, don't." But her face tipped into the cup of his palm.

He slid forward. He kissed her mouth. His hand burrowed into her hair. The scent of her surrounded him, and she kissed him back.

He moved closer still. Their kisses grew longer and deeper. He unzipped his jacket, his hand going to her waist, finding its way between her skirt and her sweater.

"So soft," he whispered as he touched her skin.

He kissed her cheek, her neck, the curve of her collarbone, pushing the sweater out of the way to kiss the tip of her shoulder.

"We can't do this," she told him in a strained voice even while she shrugged out of his jacket, moving closer, tugging his shirt from his waistband.

"We have to do this."

He touched the hem of her sweater.

She hesitated, and he waited.

She lifted her arms. He eased the sweater off, then unhooked her bra. Her breasts came free in the dash light, creamy smooth, topped with deep coral nipples. He palmed one, and then the other.

She moaned, and he pulled her to him, smoothing the heated satin of her bare back. He made a tactile memory of her shoulder, her ear, her parted lips. She drew his finger into her hot mouth, and desire ricocheted along his limbs.

Cars zipped past them on the arterial road that led to Pinion, motors whining, headlights flashing off the glass.

He kissed her again, pressing her back against the padded seat. He touched her thighs, swirling upward to her silky panties. He longed to tear them off. He was hot and hard and impatient.

Instead, he eased past their barrier, drawing them away from her, slowly peeling them down, across her thighs, her knees, her calves and over her heels. He gazed at her bare breasts.

She cradled his head, drawing him down. He kissed one pert nipple. He pushed up her skirt, his fingers parting her, feeling her heat and moisture. His breaths were labored, a rapid pulse pounding in his temple.

"You okay with this?" He forced himself to ask.

"Good." She gave a rapid nod. "Good."

He flicked the button on his pants. There was a condom in his wallet, thank goodness. He found it. He pushed his clothes out of the way, and he settled her on his lap, her legs straddling his hips.

The heat of her around him was mind-blowing. He wanted it to last. But then she moved, and he was all but lost.

He gripped her hips, planning to hold her still. "You can't."

She leaned into him, her breasts coming up against his bare chest. Her cheek went to his, and she whispered, "Watch me."

Then she flexed her hips, and he groaned loud.

"Mila, slow—"

"Too slow?"

"No."

She was going to kill him.

"Faster?"

"No. Yes." He wanted both. He wanted it all.

"I can do faster."

He tried to protest, tried to tell her, tried to explain that there was fast and then there was fast. But it all came out as a groan of despair as he fought hard for control.

"Oh, Troy." Her breathing was rapid, while whimpers started down in her chest.

He realized she meant fast. She meant very *fast*.

He stopped fighting it, letting himself go, taking over the rhythm of their lovemaking, anchoring her, going faster and harder while the headlights blurred and she cried out in ecstasy.

He followed her over the edge, his heart all but exploding with the effort. They slowed and stopped, wrapped tight in each other's arms. The heat was blasting from the car vents, and the two of them were covered in sweat.

She was limp against him, and he didn't know what to say. Should he apologize? Was she going to be angry? Disappointed?

Her hands went tight on his shoulders, and he braced himself for recriminations.

But her voice was breathy soft. "I guess we can't pretend that never happened."

Mila's breathing was still deep as she gazed at their naked bodies, latched together on the leather seat in the hazy glow of the dashboard lights. There was distorting reality, and then there was smashing it into a million pieces.

She couldn't pretend to be one of the guys when she'd just had wild, shameless sex with the boss. There was no dressing it up this time, and there was no glossing it over.

"I'm not expecting anything in return," she told him, feeling as though she needed to state that up front.

"You can have anything you want in return. Name it, and it's yours."

"That's not how I'm getting a job."

"Except a job." He softened the words with a light kiss on her neck. "I can't give you a job."

"So, anything except what I really want?" She could joke about it because she would absolutely never let him hire her that way.

"I was considering jewelry or clothes, maybe a trip. Hey, you want to take a trip? Maybe a weekend in Cancun?"

Another set of headlights flashed in the mirror. Then it stabilized, grew brighter, shining directly on the back window.

She all but leaped from Troy's lap. "Someone's stopping."

"Huh?" He swiveled to see.

"Get dressed," she called out, pulling down her skirt and

fumbling for her sweater that was wedged between the seat and the door.

At the same time, Troy yanked up his pants.

They heard a car door slam shut.

While he scrambled for his clothes, she jerked her arms into the sleeves of his jacket, stuffing her bra and panties under the seat.

Then she smoothed her hair, tucking it behind her ears.

Someone rapped on the driver's window.

Troy looked at her. He reached out to rub his thumb beneath her lower lip.

"Smeared," he said.

She quickly scrubbed her hand back and forth across her mouth and shrugged down deeper into the jacket.

Troy unrolled the window.

It was Charlie.

"You guys okay?" he asked, glancing past Troy to Mila.

She gave him what she hoped was a benign smile.

"We're fine," said Troy. "How did you do? Did you follow him home?"

Charlie straightened so Mila couldn't see his face. "I lost him at Metro Center. He parked and took the subway."

The statement surprised Mila. Had the man known he was being followed?

"He could be anywhere. I got the vehicle license. But it's registered to a numbered company. The corporate address is an abandoned building. This guy knows what he's doing."

"Can you trace it further?" Mila asked.

She was trying desperately to forget she was naked under her skirt, and that she'd just had the best sex of her life. Kassidy was what mattered here. They needed to figure out who this Jack guy was and his connection to her.

"Not tonight," said Charlie. "I'll be on it first thing tomorrow. You all okay? Car trouble?"

"We were arguing," said Troy. "The more we learn, the

more I think this has to be about me. She's convinced it's all about Kassidy."

"He's stubborn," said Mila.

"She's closed minded."

"Me?"

"Sometimes your first instinct is wrong."

"It's not wrong. It might be complex, but it's not wrong."

"Whatever," Charlie drawled. "I'll leave you to it." He gave two taps on the door and left.

Mila waited until the interior light came on in his car.

"You think he guessed?" she asked Troy.

"Guessed that you and I can't keep our hands off each other?"

"What else would I mean?"

Troy checked the rearview mirror. "Could be our incessant arguments are throwing them off."

She realized he was probably right. "Why do you suppose that is?"

"Because they think we hate each other."

"No. I mean us. I mean, how can we fight so much and then…" She pointed back and forth between them. "And then *that*?"

"Beats me," he said.

"Do you secretly like me?" The question was out before she realized how pathetic it sounded.

He didn't miss a beat. "I'm a man. I don't have to secretly like you to—" He squeezed the steering wheel, staring through the windshield. "Scrap that. Yes, I like you. I don't mean it to be a secret."

She hated how relieved she felt. She shouldn't need his validation. Sex could be sex without worrying about the whole emotional package. She certainly wasn't looking for the whole emotional package. She was only looking for a job.

"You know I'm not going to die. I'm no more likely to die than Vegas or Charlie."

He turned to look at her, genuine pain in his expression. "I can't talk about that now."

She gave a sharp nod. "Sorry. Yes. That was out of line."

"That's not what I meant."

"I'm not going to use this against you."

His voice went sharper. "That's not what I—" He stopped talking and buckled his seat belt. "It's late. Let's get you home."

She followed suit as he flipped on his signal light and pulled onto the road.

"My car's at Pinion," she reminded him.

"I'm taking you straight home."

"But—"

"No point in you having to double back at this time of night. Plus, you've been drinking."

"That was hours ago."

She didn't know why she was arguing. Why would she want to go to the Pinion office, warm up her car, then make the twenty-minute drive back to her apartment when Troy could simply drop her off?

"Shut up," he told her mildly.

"Shutting up," she agreed, leaning her head back against the seat and shutting her eyes. "Thanks."

"No problem." He made a right turn.

"You know where I live."

"I know where you live."

She'd put her address on her employment forms. But she'd had no reason to assume he'd checked them.

"Off the top of your head?" she asked.

"Off the top of my head."

"Why?"

"Because I read your file. And I'm capable of holding dozens of facts up there all at the same time."

She couldn't help but smile to herself. "Dozens?"

"Some days, I amaze myself. You know where I live. Fair's fair."

"Where you live is relevant, and it's also kind of cool."

"Cool?"

"A penthouse at the top of a fortress. I know why Kassidy feels safe there."

"She is safe there."

"I feel safe there. Then again, I also feel scrutinized when I'm there. You have a lot of cameras in that place."

"Not in the apartment."

"Thank goodness for that." She couldn't help remembering the first time they'd made love, in his office.

"Here we go." He pulled to the curb in front of her apartment building, setting the parking brake and shutting off the engine.

"Thanks," she said again. Her hand felt heavy as she reached for the door handle.

He angled his body, stretching his arm across the back of the seat. "You mind if I come up and have a look?"

The question took her by surprise.

"I'm not asking to spend the night." He glanced at his watch. "I'm getting up in three hours anyway. I just want to see where you live. I feel like you know me way better than I know you."

"Sure," she agreed.

Fair was fair. And there was no reason not to show him her apartment. In fact, she found she liked the idea. It could be that she was romanticizing the situation, but saying goodnight in her place felt better than saying it at the curb.

They walked to the front door. She inserted her key, and Troy held it open. The lobby was small—two elevators, a door to the staircase, a couple of armchairs and a planter.

Both elevators were parked at the lobby. Troy pressed the button and the doors immediately opened.

"Twelve," he said, reaching for the button.

"Did you study up on my employee forms?"

"I thought one day there'd be a quiz."

The door closed behind them.

"What else do you know about me?"

"Your weight. Your height. Your graduation date. And your mother's maiden name."

"Not my bank account numbers?"

He smirked. "Well, we did need them for direct deposit."

"I trusted you."

"You can trust me."

The doors slid open, and they began to walk again.

"I'm at the end," she said. "Or did you know that too?"

"Never took a look at the schematics."

"But you could?"

"Edison would have them for me in about five minutes."

She unlocked the apartment door, swinging it open on a living room, open kitchen and a door that led to the bedroom and bathroom.

"It's small," she warned, flicking the light switch.

He gazed around at the dove-gray sofa, the coral throw pillows, the white accent tables and the watercolor portraits. "Wow."

"Wow good or wow bad?"

"Wow, prettier than I expected."

"So, you're back to thinking I'm a girl."

"I always knew you were a girl." He stepped toward the longest row of paintings. "Who are these people?"

"I have no idea."

He turned. "You hung strangers on your wall?"

"Is that weird?"

"A little. I'd think you'd go with people you knew, or maybe celebrities or public figures."

She moved up beside him. "I like the artists. And the subjects…" She tried to put it into words. "They're people I'd like to know. Each of them strikes me as mysterious, enigmatic, someone who has a secret."

"You like secrets?"

"I like complexity. Are you hungry?" She realized she was starving. "Cookies?"

He smiled. "You have cookies?"

"Homemade, chocolate chip."

"You *baked* cookies?"

"Don't sound so surprised." She unzipped his jacket, draping it over a kitchen chair as she made her way to the cupboard.

"You definitely don't strike me as the homemaker type."

"Then aren't you learning a whole lot of new things?"

"I am."

She took the container from the bottom shelf. "I like cookies. I like them fresh. So I learned how to make them."

"Cookies sound terrific," he said.

She returned the few steps to the living room, taking a seat on the sofa and setting the cookie container on the glass-topped coffee table, removing the lid.

Troy perched beside her, peering in. "Those look great. And they smell delicious."

"Help yourself."

He did.

She took two, kicked off her shoes and curled her feet beneath her on the sofa. As she did, she remembered her underwear. It was still stuffed under the seat of his SUV.

"What?" he asked, studying her expression.

"Nothing."

"What's wrong?"

"I left some of my clothes in your car."

He did a slow blink, his expression going slightly intense. She bit down on a cookie.

"I'll get them later," he said.

She nodded.

His gaze held hers as he took a first bite.

Then his eyes lit up in surprise. "Delicious."

The reaction warmed her. "I have many talents."

"I'll say." He took another bite.

He picked out a second cookie, then he leaned back, his shoulder brushing hers. "Tell me more about your overly accomplished bombshell sister."

Mila faked an offended tone. "Hoping to do a little comparison shopping?"

"Yeah, that's what I'm doing."

"Sorry, bud. Zoey has a secret boyfriend."

"A *secret* boyfriend?" The interest level in his voice rose.

"A judge who's at odds with my mother."

"Is it serious?"

"It might be. And when the secret comes out, it's all going to hit the fan."

"It's her life," he said reasonably.

"Maybe so, but we're a close family. And they have expectations."

"That your parents get to approve your boyfriend?"

"Not exactly." She paused to think. "Well, kind of. It's important to them that we still work as a team."

"Team Stern?"

"Yes."

Troy took her hand. "You're twenty-four years old."

"You got that from my employment form."

"I did. But it's true."

She watched his thumb stroke a circular pattern on the back of her hand. She felt his light touch delve to the center of her chest, tightening her heart, making her body feel heavy and wanting.

"What's your point?" she asked.

He was silent for so long that she didn't think he was going to answer.

"No point." He cradled her head, drawing it down to rest on his shoulder. "We're going to figure this out."

"Figure what out?" From what she could tell, there was a list.

"Your life. And how it relates to mine."

Her heart stuttered then thudded. He couldn't have meant that romantically. And if he had, she should be scared. But she wasn't scared. She felt safe with Troy. The only scary part was that she wanted to keep feeling this way.

Eleven

Mila had fallen asleep in Troy's arms. And he'd held her as long as he dared before carrying her to her bed and covering her with a quilt then letting himself out of her apartment. He'd stolen a couple of extra cookies, which he now savored with a cup of coffee at the island in his kitchen.

Drake had heard Troy arrive and cried out from his crib, so he was now settled in his high chair pretending to eat cereal rounds.

"Sorry about this, bud," Troy said conversationally as he booted up his laptop to check a video he'd taken from backstage. "But you're too young for cookies."

"Bah," said Drake.

"I can't disagree with that." Troy clicked the play icon, watching closely as the man who called himself Jack made his way toward the stage at last night's performance.

"Bah, bah," said Drake, slapping his hand on the plastic tray hard enough to rattle the brackets.

"Maybe when you're older," said Troy, popping the final bite of cookie into his mouth. "If Auntie Mila is still around, she might bake you cookies."

As he said the words, Troy realized that Mila wouldn't be around to bake cookies for Drake or anyone else. Before long, she'd realize Troy was never going to give in and hire her, and she'd walk out the door.

He swallowed. The thought that she'd never forgive him left a hollow spot in his chest.

Drake let out a squeal.

"Shh." Troy put his finger to his lips. "You'll wake your mommy."

Then he paused, searching his memory, realizing he couldn't recall Kassidy ever referring to herself as "Mommy." She called Mila "Auntie Mila." But she used her own first name with Drake.

Was she struggling with the title? Was she planning to change it later? Drake deserved to have a mommy. He also deserved to have a daddy. But there wasn't anything Troy could do about that. Kassidy's career was all encompassing, and there was no sign of a boyfriend on the horizon.

He was forced to wonder all over again about Kassidy's decision. Was it too late to back out of the adoption? Might she reconsider? Of all people, Kassidy should have an appreciation for a stable family life. Theirs had been anything but.

He remembered their little house on Appleberry Street, the attic that had been converted into two bedrooms. At seven years old, Kassidy had been short enough to stand up in hers, but Troy had gotten dressed every day for high school slouched over.

Their father was always away. Kassidy's mother was off in her own world, making amateurish clay pots or writing rambling letters to the government about some perceived injustice or the other. Troy had bolted from that dysfunctional home before his graduation cap hit the ground.

Drake squealed again. He didn't seem upset or angry, more jubilant than anything else.

Troy poured another handful of cereal onto the tray in front of Drake. The majority of the rounds would end up on the floor, but they kept the little guy entertained, and usually they kept him quiet.

The video had continued playing, so Troy pulled it back to the beginning, settling in with his coffee to watch. Jack ignored the waitresses. He ignored the crowd. His attention was completely focused on Kassidy.

He could see where Mila was coming from, but he also knew he recognized the guy. And that was both significant and worrisome. The mathematical odds of a fan posing a danger to Kassidy were slim. The mathematical odds of someone from Troy's past posing a danger to his family were a whole lot higher than slim.

He took in the man's expressions, his walk, his stance.

He'd heard a little bit of the guy's voice over Mila's microphone last night, but it wasn't clear enough to gauge.

Who on earth was this guy?

"There you are, pumpkin," said Kassidy, wandering into the kitchen in a printed satin robe.

"You're up early," said Troy.

Drake squealed.

Troy smiled. "He's happy to see you."

"Of course he's happy to see me. Does he need a bottle?" Her voice changed to high-pitched baby talk. "You want Kassidy to bring you a bottle?"

"Bah," said Drake, slapping with his hand.

Troy's curiosity got the best of him. "You don't want him to call you Mommy?"

Kassidy stubbed her toe on the counter. "Ouch!"

"You okay?"

"No. Ow. Darn, that hurts." She hobbled to the table, cringing as she lowered herself into a chair.

"Are you really hurt?"

"Just give me a minute." She scrunched her eyes shut and breathed deeply.

Drake kicked his feet, squealing in a tone that sounded annoyed.

"Kassidy?"

"Yeah?"

"Don't you want Drake to call you Mommy?"

"Sure. Yes. Eventually."

"Are you having second thoughts about the adoption?"

Her eyes popped open. "No! No, Troy. I'm *not* having second thoughts. Drake is part of this family. Get *used to it.*"

Troy held his palms up in surrender.

"Can you get him?" she asked.

"Sure." Troy stopped the video and rose.

Kassidy might be frustrating, but none of this was Drake's fault. Troy unfastened the safety belt, and the baby was immediately climbing to his feet. Troy couldn't help but smile at the antics. The kid definitely knew his own mind.

Troy brushed off the stray cereal and lifted Drake into his arms.

"You're getting stronger," he told the kid.

"Bah."

"Soon I'll have to take you to the gym." Troy did a mock exercise with Drake's chubby arm. "I'm a pretty good drill sergeant. You'll be buff enough to get any girl you want."

Troy's thoughts turned to Mila, her struggles on the obstacle course. Her killer naked body wrapped around his.

"Then again," he said quietly, "sometimes the girl's buff enough to get you."

Drake tugged at Troy's lower lip.

"Can you picture it?" asked Kassidy.

Troy stared at his sister. Did she know what he was talking about? Had she guessed that he was powerless to resist Mila?

"What?" he asked cautiously, hoping he could come up with an explanation on the fly.

"The gym, with Drake, when he's older. Do you see yourself in his life?"

Troy felt a rush of relief. "Sure. Why not? If he doesn't have a daddy around, he's going to need me."

Kassidy blinked rapidly, her eyes shimmering with tears.

"Hey," Troy cooed. "What's this?" He moved to her.

"My toe," she answered, her voice thick. "No, it's not my toe. It's you, Troy. You're stepping up."

Troy hoisted the wiggly Drake. "You mean with this little guy?"

"Yes."

"I'll admit, I don't know what you're doing. I'm not sure it's the right thing. But I'll be here for you, Kassidy." He thought back again to the house on Appleberry. She'd been so incredibly young back then. "I probably should have been here for you a long time ago."

She shook her head, coming to her feet, unexpectedly

wrapping her arms around him. "You're here for us now, big brother. That's all that counts."

"I'm here for you now," he said, wrapping his free arm around her.

Mila woke up alone on top of her bed, still dressed in Kassidy's clothes, a comforter keeping her warm. It was nearly ten o'clock in the morning, and she had no idea how late Troy had stayed. He'd obviously carried her to the bed. The realization was both heartwarming and unnerving.

She wondered if he'd slept at all. She was guessing not. He was probably chasing down leads for his own pet theory, which meant she was already running behind on her work. Would he hold it against her? Would he see her falling asleep as a sign of female weakness?

She swung her legs off the bed and headed for the shower. She needed to redeem herself, to demonstrate her analytical abilities, to remind him she was more than just a good-time girl.

She twisted the shower taps to full and stepped into the spray. Last night had been a mistake. And she knew she should regret it more.

Okay, she should find a way to regret it at all. Because she didn't. Right now, making love with Troy was a warm, exotic memory. Forget regret—she wanted to do it all over again.

This was bad. It was terrible. She might have undone every bit of her hard work. Nobody was going to take her seriously now, least of all Troy. And if he told anyone else—

She felt suddenly cold. *Would* he tell anyone? Would he tell Vegas?

Vegas was her best ally at Pinion, and she'd promised him she wouldn't sleep with Troy. If Vegas lost faith in her, if he thought she was fickle, if he thought she was weak—

She groaned under the hot spray. She'd worked hard for this chance. She wanted to be strong and in control, to take on both physical and mental challenges. She wanted to work with a top team and keep others safe. But the chance was rapidly slipping from her grasp. She had to stop the slide.

She squirted some shampoo into her palm, pushing her brain back to Kassidy and Drake, and back to Jack.

Troy would be looking at the man's connection to himself. It followed that his staff would be looking there, too. Mila needed to come at it from Kassidy, or even from Drake.

Suds running down her neck, her earlier theory came to mind again. It was outlandish, but it wasn't impossible. Jack could be Drake's father. Kassidy might not even know.

She hadn't reacted to the picture of Jack. But she'd sure reacted to the question of Drake's father. Maybe she knew Drake's father was dangerous, but maybe she didn't know who he was.

A chill came over her. If that was true, she needed concrete evidence to take to Troy. Because if she was right, they needed to protect Drake as much as they needed to protect Kassidy.

She threw on a pair of jeans and a T-shirt. Her car was still at Pinion, but she didn't have any time to waste. She hailed a cab and went directly to the airport. She didn't have much to go on, only the name of the hospital and Drake's date of birth.

She'd try the hospital first. If that didn't work, she'd go to public records. She might be able to talk her way into getting at least partial details.

It took her two hours to get to New Jersey, and less than ten minutes to get shut down by the hospital staff. By midafternoon, she was fighting a losing battle with the department of vital statistics. Without parental permission, she was not getting her hands on Drake's birth certificate.

She tried to explain that his mother was dead, and his father was unknown. She even pretended the query was related to Kassidy's adoption, hoping they'd have Kassidy's name on file. She was told to get a lawyer and a court order.

Defeated, she left the building, pausing on the stone steps, traffic whizzing through the intersection in front of her.

"Problem?" asked a well-dressed man in his late thirties.

He moved up the steps toward her, flashing a friendly smile.

"No problem." She looked away.

"Get what you were looking for?"

"I did," she answered, starting to walk.

He fell into step beside her. "It doesn't look like you did."

"And what exactly would that look like?" As soon as the question was out, she wanted to kick herself. She'd just played into his hand.

"You wouldn't look so defeated. You'd have kept walking."

"I am walking."

"And you'd be carrying a manila envelope." He nodded to a couple who were also exiting the building. "Like that one."

"It's in my purse."

"Your purse isn't big enough. My name's Hank Meyer. I might be able to help you out. For a small fee, of course."

"I'm not interested, Mr. Meyer."

"Call me Hank."

"I don't believe I will." She picked up her pace.

"There are other ways of getting records."

Mila held up her hand to hail a cab. "Illegal ways?"

The guy was either fleecing her or asking her to participate in the crime.

"Quasi-legal."

"There's no such thing as quasi-legal."

He pointed across the street. "There's an internet café right there on the corner. They take cash. You're in, you're out, there's not a single footprint."

"It's still illegal."

"They're called opaque records. You can see them. You can't download them. You can't use them for any business or personal purpose. But you can snap a screenshot with your cell phone."

A yellow taxi passed by, but it already had a passenger.

"What are you looking for?" asked Hank Meyer.

"None of your business."

"I'm only trying to help you."

"No, you're not."

He had an angle. She just hadn't figured out what it was yet. An internet café was public, so she'd be in no physical danger. And using cash protected her identity and credit cards—his most likely scam. Perhaps this was bait and switch. It started out with cash, but then a credit card was ultimately required.

Another cab came into view, and she waved at it.

"You don't like what I have to offer, you can walk away at any time."

She sighed in exasperation as the cab passed by. "You're wasting your time, Mr. Meyer. I'm not falling for it."

"What were you after?"

She frowned at him.

"Just in broad strokes. Birth, death, divorce? I can tell you're on the job."

"On the job?"

"A private investigator."

"I'm not... Okay, I am investigating."

"Then you're either young or new. You look like you're both. We walk across the street. You give me the name. Fifty bucks, you're in, you're out. It's not exactly legal, but nobody's throwing anybody in jail if you're caught. Scratch that. If I'm caught, maybe I get a fine. You're just an innocent bystander."

"Or maybe you're law enforcement and, by the way, this is entrapment."

He laughed at that. "Yeah. Plainclothes detectives deployed to the public records center to entrap otherwise law-abiding document thieves. Now that's a good use of public resources."

Mila hated to admit that he had a point. She also hated to admit she was tempted. Fifty dollars. For fifty dollars could she get a sneak peek at Drake's birth certificate?

"This is Jersey, ma'am. Believe me when I tell you law enforcement has way better things to do."

Another cab sailed past. Mila couldn't help but wonder if it was a sign. She couldn't see any genuine dangers in the man's offer. He was likely just trying to make quick money.

"Have you been doing this long?" she asked.

"Two years. Never had a problem. What kind of a record?"

"Birth certificate."

"Recent?"

"This year."

"Piece of cake." He gestured to the crosswalk.

She took a bracing breath. "All right, Mr. Meyer. But I should tell you I have a black belt in Krav Maga and a permit to carry concealed."

"I don't expect the computer to fight back," he said easily. "But good to know."

The walk signal changed, and Mila quickly stepped up. If she was going to do this, she'd rather get it over with.

She gave Drake's name, birth date and the hospital information to Meyer. Then she waited on the sidewalk, feeling like a convenience store robber. Thankfully, he was back quickly.

"Start walking," he told her.

"Did you get caught?"

He grinned. "No. I'm done, that's all. Do you need a copy? It's safer if you just look at it on my phone, then there's no digital link between us. But if you need me to send it—"

"I'll just look," she said.

"Smart." He handed her his phone.

She looked at the photo, and her heart stopped.

She looked up at him, wondering if this could be some colossal con or sick joke.

"What?" He looked genuinely concerned. "Are you okay?"

"This is it?"

"Absolutely." He pointed to Drake's name and then to his birthdate.

"It's…" She didn't know what to say.

"Fifty bucks," he reminded her.

"Yes. Yes." She dug into her pocket, extracting the fifty she'd placed there while he was in the internet café. "Thank you."

"Pleasure doing business with you." He took his phone and sauntered away.

Mila moved down the sidewalk, gripping an iron fence at the edge of a small park.

It was Troy.

Troy was Drake's biological father.

She had to call Kassidy. And Kassidy *had* to talk to Troy.

What on *earth* was the woman doing? And who was out there stalking her?

"Kassidy is shopping with Mila," said Troy. He was on his way up from the Pinion garage, back from a working lunch with the Bulgarian planning team. "I told her she could turn the extra bedroom into a nursery." He couldn't help but smile at the memory. "She was really excited."

"Mila's car is still here," said Vegas.

"That's weird." Troy had assumed Mila would grab a cab back to the office once she woke up.

Again, he smiled, remembering how peaceful she'd looked when he'd left her, remembering how she had felt sleeping in his arms. He knew he was going to have to figure this all out, and soon. But for a moment he just wanted to enjoy how close he felt to her.

"The nanny's here, and Kassidy's late."

"So call her."

"Gabby tried, but she kept getting voice mail."

"Did you try?"

"For the past hour. Same thing."

Troy paused, for the first time hearing the worry in Vegas's voice. "You think something's going on?"

"I think we can't locate Kassidy, and she's been out of touch for a few hours."

"Call Mila."

The women had to be together. It was the only thing that made sense. Kassidy wanted to decorate the nursery right away. She couldn't wait to pick out wallpaper and furniture.

"I've tried Mila," said Vegas.

"Where are you?"

"The office."

"On my way up. I'll try Mila myself." Troy stabbed the end button as he mounted the stairs.

He dialed Mila, but it went straight to voice mail. He left a terse message to call him. She shouldn't be out of touch like this. Did she need call-waiting? They'd buy her call-waiting.

He strode down the hallway, thinking his way through the situation.

"Does Mila still have her communications device from last night?" he asked Vegas. "Get Edison to ping it."

Vegas immediately called down to Edison.

Troy greeted Gabby, who was in the office with Vegas. "I take it Kassidy was supposed to be here?"

"Over an hour ago," said Gabby. "Usually she calls if plans change."

"When did you last talk to her?"

"Last night."

So Troy was probably the last one to see his sister that morning.

"Do you mind waiting in the apartment?" he asked Gabby. "If she calls or shows up, get her to contact me right away."

"Of course," said Gabby. "If there's anything I can do to help."

"That's the biggest help you can be."

"I'm sure there's a simple explanation."

"So am I," said Troy, believing it less and less as the minutes ticked past.

"Mila's earwig is in her apartment," Vegas said as Gabby left the office.

Troy's phone buzzed, and he quickly checked the display.

"Mila," he said to Vegas, putting it to his ear. "Where are you?" he demanded.

"Getting in a cab. I'm on my way to the office."

"Kassidy's with you?"

"No. I haven't been able to reach her. Why?"

"You're not shopping?"

"I had something I needed to check out."

Troy swore.

"What happened?" Mila sounded worried.

"We don't know. Kassidy's out of touch."

"How long?" Mila's voice went on alert.

"At least an hour, maybe more. We thought she was with you."

"I haven't seen her since last night. Listen, there's something going on here that we haven't—"

"Who on earth *is* that guy?" Troy had racked his brain to no avail. His fuzzy memory of Jack was the best lead they had. "I have to call Charlie."

"Sure." Mila paused. "I'll be there in ten minutes."

"Good."

Troy wasn't sure why he felt relieved at the thought of her presence. There wasn't anything Mila could do to help. Kassidy might still be safe. She might have gone shopping alone and had her phone battery die.

And if that wasn't the case, if something had happened to her, there was nothing Mila could do that the Pinion team wouldn't already have underway.

"Yes, boss?" came Charlie's voice on the phone.

"What did you find out about the numbered company?"

"Not much. It's hidden behind a holding company."

"Local or offshore?" The thought that this could be an international client made things even more urgent.

"Pennsylvania."

That news was a relief—a small relief. It meant it likely wasn't a violent enemy based out of South America or the Middle East.

"Lancaster," said Charlie. "Didn't you live there once?"

"Yes," said Troy. He'd lived there with his father, Kassidy's mother and Kassidy. Adrenaline suddenly slammed the truth into his system. "Ronnie Hart."

Vegas looked up sharply.

"Who's that?" asked Charlie.

Troy's hair stood on end. "Find me Ronnie Hart. Anything you can get." Troy's brain started to race. "Particularly real estate. Does he own or rent anything in DC, Maryland or Virginia?"

"On it. That's our guy?"

"He's our guy," said Troy, ending the call.

"What?" asked Vegas, coming to his feet.

"A neighbor." Troy blew out a breath, not sure whether to be relieved or terrified. "Ronnie Hart was a neighbor on Appleberry Street, a teenager back then. But he played with Kassidy. He really seemed to like her. She was only seven, and it was kind of odd, but I was too self-absorbed to pay any attention. Her mother and my father were in their own worlds. You know, the kid practically raised herself."

"He's got them," said Vegas, tucking a gun into the back of his pants.

Troy agreed. "It wasn't about me."

He desperately scrambled for memories. Was Ronnie dangerous or merely deluded? He wasn't an international criminal bent on revenge. But he sure wasn't in touch with reality, either.

Vegas hooked up his earwig, tossing one to Troy. "Let's go get them."

Mila burst through the doorway. "What do we know?"

"Ronnie Hart," said Troy, gearing up himself.

"You have a name?"

"A former neighbor of Kassidy's and mine. Looking back,

I recognize the seeds of obsession. He must have followed her here. And now he's probably kidnapped them."

Mila moved closer, voice going low. "I need to talk to you."

"You armed?"

"Yes. But, Troy, we need to talk."

"Not now. Edison is looking for an address. I want to be in the car when he gets it."

"Now," said Mila. "Right now."

Troy glared at her. There was nothing more important than finding Kassidy and Drake. Whatever she wanted to hash out between them could wait.

"Mila," Vegas called. He tossed her an earwig. "You're coming?"

"I'm coming," said Mila. "Two minutes," she said to Troy, her voice implacable.

"I'll get Charlie and meet you in the garage," said Vegas.

"What is *your problem*?" Troy demanded as the door closed behind his partner.

"I'm sorry to do this," said Mila.

"Then *do it* later." Troy took his phone in hand, ready to answer the second Edison called.

"I wanted to talk to Kassidy first."

Troy gritted his teeth, his muscles turning to iron with anxiety and frustration.

"It's Drake," said Mila. "I'm sorry to say it like this. But, Troy, he's your son."

The words didn't make sense. They made absolutely no sense whatsoever. His first thought was that it was a joke. But if Mila was joking right now, he'd throw her out on her ass.

"Drake's mother is Julie Fortune."

Troy staggered on his feet, and a roar came up in his ears. "Julie?"

"You knew her?"

"She was a backup singer. For Kassidy."

"And…"

"It was one night." He barely remembered it. "In New York last year."

His brain scrambled through the memory. The dates were right. And Julie and Kassidy seemed to be close. The pieces became instantly clear. Troy had a son. Drake was his son. His son was in peril.

"Troy?" Mila touched his arm.

He forcibly snapped himself out of it. "Let's go."

A million thoughts pounded his brain as he strode through to the garage. But he couldn't let it mess with his judgment. He had a job to do.

As he entered the garage, his phone finally rang.

"Yeah?"

"Good call, boss," said Edison. "Ronnie Hart owns a house in Virginia. I just sent the address to your phones and to the vehicle GPS system. It'll take twenty minutes to get there."

"Get our earwigs all up on communications."

"Doing that right now."

"Over and out," Troy said, breaking into a run.

Twelve

It was an unassuming house, a single-story bungalow, red brick with black shutters on a corner lot of a quiet street. They'd parked two blocks away. Charlie and Vegas took the back, while Mila and Troy approached from the street.

Brown leaves were scattered on the lawn. Two maple trees and some miniature shrubs offered little in the way of concealment, so they stayed to one side of the building.

"Hang back," Troy told her.

"Yeah, right," she scoffed.

Mila was using every ounce of her skill and training to make sure Kassidy and Drake came out of this uninjured.

"That's an order."

"What are you going to do, fire me?"

He glared at her.

"Wait, listen." Her stomach clenched. "Oh, man."

It was a baby crying. Drake was inside that house crying his eyes out in fear, possibly hunger.

"It's a good thing," said Troy, his body taut, eyes steely with concentration.

"I know."

It meant Drake was okay for now.

They came to a stop, crouched under a window. And Troy stood slowly to look inside.

"It's a bedroom," he whispered to her and to everyone on the communications system. "I can't see anyone."

"They're not in the kitchen," said Vegas.

"Drake sounds like he's in the living room," said Mila.

Nobody disputed the analysis.

"You want to storm it?" asked Charlie.

"Too much of a risk," said Troy.

"Let me knock on the door," Mila suggested.

"Why you?" asked Vegas.

"I look normal. The rest of you look like mercenaries."

"Bad plan," said Troy. "He'll recognize you from the club."

"He didn't pay that much attention," she countered. "And I looked pretty different last night."

Nobody said anything.

"Got a better plan?" she asked.

"Stealth," said Vegas. "I can pick the lock on the back door."

"I'm going to check the living room window," said Troy.

He motioned for Mila to stay put, then he crept along the front of the house, below the level of the windows.

She followed anyway.

"It's only a matter of time before the neighbors see us and call the cops," she said.

He looked back at her and scowled.

"She's right," said Charlie. "If the cops show up, we could have a bad hostage situation."

Troy rose slowly, peeping into the front window. Then he snapped back down. "They're in there. But they're too close together. If we storm it, we risk Kassidy and Drake." He looked at Mila.

"Stealth's not an option?" asked Vegas.

"Any sound and he might grab one of them."

"I can do it," said Mila, making up her mind. "I'll knock. I'm just a woman with car trouble and a broken cell phone. If I get in, I can separate them and buy you some time."

There was another silence.

"Best we got," said Vegas.

Troy stared hard at Mila, looking as though he was trying to see down to her soul. He wanted to know she could pull it off.

She held her hand out flat, showing him her nerves were steady.

"Okay," he agreed.

He took up a spot between two windows, flattening himself against the wall. "No unnecessary chances."

"I'll only take the necessary ones." She tucked her gun into the back of her pants, moved her hair so that it covered her earpiece, then marched up the three concrete steps to the front door.

She boldly pushed the doorbell and knocked loudly, trying to sound like someone who wouldn't easily go away.

"Hello?" she called. "Hello? I need some help out here."

She glanced at Troy as she waited.

His mind had to be reeling from both the situation and the revelation about Drake. But he looked stoic, professional, focused. The job was the job, and he was getting it done.

This was why she admired him, she realized. It was why she wanted to learn from him. It was why she was falling for him.

She forcibly banished the distracting thought, banging on the door again. "Hello? I need to borrow your phone."

Drake was still crying inside, and she couldn't hear anything else.

She cupped her hand over the small opaque window, making a show of peering inside. "My car's broken down."

"Come on," she muttered under her breath. "Open up."

Then the door cracked. "I can't help you."

"I'm so sorry to bother you," she rushed on. "I hope I didn't wake your baby. How old is he, by the way? I have a niece."

"You need to leave," said Ronnie Hart.

"I understand. I will. But you're the third house I've tried, and nobody's home. I've got an appointment. I'm meeting my sister. She's pregnant. It's an ultrasound. It might be twins. And I just need to get the auto club. *Please?*"

It took him a minute to answer. "What's their number?"

"Oh, you're a lifesaver." She made a show of digging into her pocket. Then she leaned suddenly on the door, popping it open, sending him stumbling back.

"Thanks so much." she said, pretending he'd opened the door himself.

He swiftly backed away, placing himself next to Kassidy. She was pale and shaking. She seemed emotionally wrung out, holding a crying Drake and looking as if she might drop him.

"Hi, there," Mila told her cheerfully, making eye contact, hoping against hope she wouldn't react. "Nice to meet you. Cute kid. Your husband is making a call for me."

Thank goodness, Kassidy kept quiet.

But Ronnie took Drake from her arms. Not good.

"I know the number's here somewhere."

She looked up, and Ronnie was holding a gun on Kassidy.

"What's with the gun?" she asked to alert Troy and the others.

"Move!" Troy ordered.

"I recognize you now." Ronnie sneered at her. "You were there last night, chatting me up. You two must be friends."

Troy moved cautiously through the doorway, his gun drawn, gaze pinned on Ronnie.

"Back off," Ronnie ordered. He cocked the pistol. "Tell the other two to stay in the kitchen."

Troy's gaze went to Vegas and Charlie.

"I mean it!" Ronnie shouted. His eyes were glazed, and his face was flushed. He dangled the crying Drake precariously under one arm, the gun in his other hand trained on Kassidy, who was only inches away.

"Stay back," said Troy, motioning to Vegas and Charlie.

"We know what's going on here," said Mila in the calmest tone she could muster.

Ronnie brushed the gun against Kassidy's temple.

"I know you like Kassidy. I like her, too." Mila tried a smile.

"You know *nothing*," Ronnie spat.

"Mila," Troy warned.

But she couldn't back off. She was closest to them, and she was the only one who didn't have a gun trained on him. She needed to keep his attention, stop him from fixating on the deadliness of the situation and keep him from deciding he had nothing left to lose. And she needed to send a signal to Kassidy.

"I love her singing," said Mila, shifting her weight and using the movement to propel herself forward. "You must love it a lot. I know you've been in the audience.

"She's working on a new song," Mila continued. "With some great dance moves." She did a couple of foot moves, using the momentum to take her even closer to them.

Then she looked hard at Kassidy, peering deep into her eyes, willing her to understand the message. "There's this one move."

"Shut up!" Ronnie cried.

She continued staring at Kassidy. "At the opening of the new song. It's quite spectacular."

Kassidy's eyes went wide, and the blood drained from her face.

"We should get her to do it."

"Everybody," shouted Ronnie. "Get out!" He shook Drake, who shrieked in terror.

Two big tears welled up in Kassidy's eyes.

"Now!" Mila yelled, diving through the air for Drake.

Kassidy dropped to the ground. The gun went off. Mila tore Drake from Ronnie's arms, spinning her body to land on her back and break his fall.

She ripped the gun from her waistband and trained it on Ronnie.

But Troy was already there. He had Ronnie pinned to the floor. He flipped him over, fastening his wrists together.

Vegas was lifting Kassidy, cradling her in his arms.

"Get her out of here." Troy's voice was hoarse.

"Everybody okay?" asked Mila, gun still pointed at Ronnie.

Troy stared at her. She couldn't tell if he was angry or relieved.

Vegas carried Kassidy out the front door, while sirens sounded and grew louder. Obviously, the neighbors had reacted to the disturbance.

"I'll take him," Charlie said to Mila, crouching to lift Drake from her chest.

"He sounds hungry," said Mila, glancing around. "See if Kassidy had a diaper bag."

"Seriously?" asked Charlie.

"Seriously," said Mila.

Babies' stomachs didn't know anything about hostage-taking incidents. And with all that crying, he was probably dehydrated.

"I'm not changing his diaper," said Charlie.

"Wimp," said Troy, hauling Ronnie roughly to his feet.

Hours later, Ronnie was in custody, Drake was fast asleep and Troy was desperately trying to make sense of his life.

In the dimly lit bedroom, he smoothed his palm over his son's silky hair, watching his little chest rise and fall beneath the powder-blue sleeper. Drake suckled in his sleep, his red lips pursing in a bow. His fingers wriggled and so did his toes. Troy couldn't fathom what a baby that young could possibly dream about.

He also couldn't fathom what miracle had brought him here. How had Troy ended up with a child? He was the last person in the world who deserved an innocent baby. He had no role models to draw on. He had an erratic, sometimes dangerous job. He hadn't read any books, done any research. He certainly hadn't done any of the work to get Drake to this point in his little life.

"You drew the short straw, buddy," he whispered, his voice unexpectedly breaking.

Damn.

"But you're here," Troy continued. "And I'm what you get. And we're going to make the best of it. Okay?"

He leaned down and gave Drake a kiss on the cheek.

He straightened. "Okay." He braced himself. "Okay, that's what we're going to do."

He could hear Mila's and Kassidy's voices murmuring in the living room. A doctor had checked out his sister. She'd been suffering from mild shock, but some dinner and a glass of wine seemed to help.

Now he needed to talk to her. He needed about a million questions answered. Their voices grew louder as he entered the room.

He stopped. He stared in disbelief at his sneaky sister, reflexively folding his arms over his chest.

"Troy," said Mila in a warning tone. "The interrogation can wait."

"I don't think so." He moved forward, taking one of the armchairs, cornerwise from Kassidy.

He knew he had to stay calm. She'd had an incredibly rough day. But he needed answers.

"I don't get it," he said to his sister. "Why the ruse? Why not tell me up front?"

Kassidy's voice shook a little. "I wasn't sure how."

He felt like a heel, but he couldn't back off.

"Honestly," she said. "I wasn't sure *if* I should tell you at all. I know you don't want a baby."

"It doesn't matter if I want a baby or not. I *have* a baby."

"Troy, take it easy," said Mila.

"Julie asked me to adopt him. She wanted him to stay with his family."

Troy guessed he could understand that.

"I was afraid." Kassidy swallowed. "I was afraid you'd give him away."

Troy opened his mouth to protest.

"No," she said. "I knew there was a chance you wouldn't want him. And I know you thought I'd make a terrible mother."

He couldn't argue that. When she'd first showed up on his doorstep with Drake, that was exactly what he'd thought.

"I was terrified." Her throat sounded clogged. "That you'd make me give him away to someone better. But I love him, Troy. I was there when he was born. I couldn't bear to give him to strangers."

Troy's chest tightened. "We're not giving him to strangers." He leaned out to take her hand. "He's my son, Kassidy. Of course I'm going to raise my son."

She gave him a watery smile. Beside her, Mila wiped her eyes with the back of her hand.

Troy wanted to smile at that. Mila had been a rock today, and now she was getting sappy over a little baby. He swallowed a lump of emotion himself. He supposed he understood.

"You did good today," he told Kassidy. "Really good. You kept your cool and helped save Drake's life."

A shudder visibly ran though her. He realized she was still pale, and there were shadows under her eyes.

"Get some sleep," he told her. "We've got a nursery to plan."

She managed a smile.

"And your room, too. I want you here as much as possible to help with Drake."

She gave a rapid nod.

"We're an unorthodox family." That was an understatement. "But we are a family."

"We can do better than we have in the past," she said.

"Absolutely," Troy agreed.

Kassidy slowly rose to her feet. "Okay. That's good. I'm going to bed now." She leaned over to give Mila a hug. "Thank you *so* much."

"Get some sleep."

"I will." Kassidy gave a chopped sigh and left for her bedroom.

His gaze came to rest on Mila.

She looked back.

"You want to talk now?" he asked, even as his energy drained silently away.

"Are you ticked off at me?"

"Little bit."

She'd taken an incredible risk. She'd ignored his direct

orders in the field. They'd had a good outcome, but the end didn't always justify the means. And the end could have been very different.

"Then, no," she said. "I don't want to talk right now."

But she surprised him by rising, crossing the room and setting herself down in his lap.

His entire body sang in contentment. He settled an arm around her shoulders.

She peeled off her shoes. "Let's argue later."

"Later works for me." He had no desire to argue with her just then.

She leaned her head against his shoulder, and he placed his palm on her warm stomach. She was so fit and tough, but she was still soft and smooth. How could anyone be such a perfect combination?

The curve of her backside was cradled in his lap, and it took about thirty seconds for his body to respond.

He rested his cheek against her hair and inhaled deeply.

"I know we always do this impulsively," he said. "We don't analyze it, and we don't discuss it. But I have to say, all relevant facts considered, I really want to carry you off to my bedroom and make love to you for the next twelve hours or so."

"Maybe we should discuss the pros and cons," she whispered.

"There are a lot of pros." He wrapped his hand around her rib cage and settled her more closely to his body.

"Such as?"

"Such as, you're beautiful, you're soft and sexy, you're smart and funny and bold as all get-out. And I love the way you smell."

She turned her face toward him. "I love the way you smell." Her palms slid up his chest. "And I love the way you feel. So strong. You make me feel safe."

"You are safe."

She tilted her chin, and he kissed her mouth. She tasted amazing. He kissed her again.

"There are also cons."

"Not tonight. The cons can sit this one out. The world can sit this one out. It's just you and me, Mila."

She smiled, her green eyes bright and deep as a glacial lake. "Okay."

She pushed herself up and stood.

He took her hand. She snagged the bottle of wine.

On the way past the bar, he picked up a couple of glasses.

He locked the bedroom door behind them, hitting the switch for the gas fireplace. The spacious room was filled with a soft orange glow.

"Nice," she said.

"You're what's nice."

He set down the wine and the glasses and pulled back the covers on the king-size bed.

She followed him over, removing her T-shirt and dispensing with her bra. He pulled off his own shirt, unbuttoning his pants. Then he paused while she stripped off her socks and her jeans and stood there in her white lace panties.

"You're gorgeous," he told her, tracing a line from her neck to her shoulder and down her arm. "Can I just stand here and look at you for a while?"

"Sure," she said.

He'd expected to be impatient. He was definitely aroused. But he didn't just want sex here. He wanted more. He wanted to know her like nobody else knew her. He wanted all of her, body and soul.

She traced a scar that traversed his abdomen. He knew it was the most prominent one. She looked expectantly up at him.

"Car crash. Chasing a guy through downtown Munich."

"Not a knife fight?"

"Knife fights are bad news. You want to stay out of knife fights."

"Did you catch him?" she asked.

"I did."

She traced another scar.

"My misspent youth," he told her.

"Poor baby." She leaned in to kiss it.

The warmth of her lips sent tendrils of desire skittering across his skin. He groaned and drew her into his arms.

"You feel even better than you look," he said.

"So do you."

"Kiss me."

She looked up at him. "Sure."

He brought his lips to hers, and the world truly did fall away. He lifted her onto the bed, stripped off the rest of his clothes, dispensed with her panties and drew her full-length into his arms. She was all limbs and motion, warmth and friction. He touched her everywhere, kissed her everywhere, watched the firelight play off the honey of her skin.

She was everything he wasn't. Her hair was soft as silk. Her lips were like rose petals. Her soft breasts filled his hands, and her moist body welcomed him into the apex of heat and softness. He wanted to stay here forever. He wanted Mila forever.

There was no way in the world he could see giving her up.

Finally, they were satiated and still. He lay there beside her, then rose up on one elbow to gaze at her. Her eyes were closed. Her breathing was even. If she wasn't asleep, she soon would be.

He was in love with her.

He'd never felt it before, but he was certain of it. He wanted everything for her, nothing but the best. He wanted her to be happy and safe, and he wanted her to be close to him—to him and Drake—forever.

He didn't know what to do about that, but there it was.

"You saved my son," he whispered.

"Hmm?" The word was barely a breath. Her hand twitched but then went still.

"Thank you, Mila."

* * *

Mila awoke feeling lighter and more confident. She emerged from Troy's bedroom, hearing his voice coming from the kitchen. It was obvious he was talking to Drake.

She stopped in the doorway, leaning on the wall. "Morning."

Troy smiled at the sound of her voice, looking up from his tablet. "Morning."

She walked into the room.

"Coffee?" he asked.

"Love some."

He rose to take a white mug from the bottom shelf. "Sleep well?"

"I did." She stroked the top of Drake's head.

He banged his heels against the high chair, selecting another round of cereal.

"Me, too." Troy handed her a cup of coffee.

"You want to say what you've got to say?" she asked.

She'd ignored his orders last night, and he had a right to be annoyed. He'd said as much before they'd made love last night.

"It's over," he said.

"I don't understand."

Didn't he want to lay down the law, tell her to never pull anything like that again?

"Let's move on."

"To what?" She didn't want special treatment. If she deserved a dressing-down, she'd take it.

"Last night," he said, his voice gentle, hand coming up to touch her cheek, "well, it made me realize…"

"That I can hack it?"

"That you're one in a million."

Her heart warmed. "So, you get it now? You see what I can do."

He gave a secretive smile, stepping closer. "I saw what you can do, all right."

"That's not what I meant."

"It was pretty fantastic."

She wrapped her hand around his wrist. "I meant on the job."

"Let's not talk about the job."

She took a step back. "I proved my point."

His voice firmed up. "That it wasn't about me? I did know Ronnie Hart."

"What? No. I'm not saying you were wrong. I'm saying I handled myself. I did the job. I *saved* Drake."

Troy's voice went flat. "You're saying you want to be rewarded?"

"To be acknowledged. I want what I've always wanted, Troy."

His hand dropped to his side. "A hundred guys could have done what you did."

It took her a minute to believe he'd said it.

"You're better than that, Mila. You're more than those hundred guys put together."

She stared hard at his implacable expression. "Oh, no, you don't. Don't you dare tell me I'm too good for you to hire."

"You are too good for me to hire. I want you in my life, not as some employee, as a woman, as the woman—"

"No," Mila cried out.

He couldn't do this. He wouldn't do this.

"Hear me out," he said.

Dread trickled through her. "What about last night?"

"Last night had nothing to do with any job."

"But—"

His expression turned sour. "You said you'd never sleep your way into a job."

She wasn't talking about the sex. She was talking about rescuing Drake and Kassidy. "I showed you what I can do. I proved to you I was just as good as any man."

"Did I ever, even once say I wanted you to prove something? Did I ever offer to hire you? Did I ever give you any false hope?"

"I thought…" She'd thought he'd come around. She'd thought after yesterday he'd be forced to see she could do it.

Drake kicked and vocalized in the background, tossing cereal rounds to the floor.

"I want you in my life, Mila," said Troy.

"But not in your company."

"I want you forever, not just until the first bullet—" He abruptly stopped, balling his hands into fists.

"You have no faith in me."

"I'm a realist. I can't pretend I'm not."

She set down her cup and backed for the door. "And I can't pretend I'm a failure."

"I never said—"

"I'm not a failure, Troy." A sharp pain gripped her chest, tightening in the hollow space around her heart.

She'd deluded herself. She thought because she loved him, he loved her back. And if he loved her, he had to respect her.

She was wrong. He'd never respect her. Nothing had changed. He would never change.

It was over. She might be a Stern, but she'd failed anyway. She'd absolutely failed.

"Why didn't you *tell me*?" Troy demanded, glaring at Vegas's back where he sat in the control room.

"Tell you what?" Vegas asked without turning.

"That she was here. That she came back."

Troy's world had functionally ended two weeks ago when Mila walked out. He went through his days by rote, missing her every single second.

"She's been back a bunch of times," said Vegas.

"What?" Troy stared at the monitor that was trained on the obstacle course where Mila was dragging herself through the mud.

Vegas turned in his swivel chair. "To practice. She never gave up on herself. She's hell-bent on finishing it."

Resentment rose in Troy, anger at Vegas for keeping him in the dark. "Who else knows?"

"Everyone."

Troy saw red. He didn't dare speak. He wanted to fire the entire company.

"They've helped her," said Vegas. "Charlie, Edison, me. We've all shared our best techniques."

"Nobody goes near her," Troy shouted. *"Nobody."*

"Boss?" Charlie asked from behind him.

"Better get out of here," warned Vegas.

"Why?" asked Charlie.

Then Troy faced him, and Charlie's eyes went wide.

"What were you doing with Mila?" Troy demanded.

Charlie held his palms up in surrender, backing into the hall. "Nothing. Nothing, boss. I just gave her a few pointers on the obstacle course."

"They like her," said Vegas.

"I like her, too," Troy shouted. "That's why I want to keep her alive."

"She's not going to die," Vegas stated with impatience.

"Not on my watch," said Troy.

"She's no more likely to die than you," said Charlie.

Troy all but growled at him.

But Charlie took a bold step forward. "You're wrong in this."

"That's *not* your call."

Had Charlie lost his mind?

"Can Vegas take you?" Charlie asked. "Hand to hand, can he not take you every single time?"

Troy wasn't walking into that trap. It wasn't the same thing.

"Does that make you useless?" asked Charlie.

"Watch your—"

"Take me?" Charlie spoke right over Troy. "I'm not that big. But I can shoot a gnat from five hundred yards. And Edison? Even I can take Edison. But give him some common cleaning products and a remote car starter and he'll level a city block."

"It's *not* the same thing," Troy ground out.

"It's exactly the same thing," said Charlie. He pointed to the video monitor. "We like her. We *need* her. Diversity makes us stronger, and we want her on the team. We voted."

"You *voted*?" Troy couldn't believe what he was hearing.

"It was unanimous."

"Since when does voting have anything to do with decisions at Pinion?"

"I certainly have a vote," Vegas said quietly.

Troy and Charlie turned to look at him.

"But you're wrong if you think it's the same thing," Vegas said to Charlie.

Troy was supremely thankful for Vegas's sanity.

"It's different with Mila," Vegas continued. "It's different because Troy's not in love with you, or with me, or with Edison."

"I'm not—" Troy stopped himself. Did he really want to deny it out loud?

"Here's the thing," Vegas said to Troy. "You can love all of her, or you can love none of her. You don't get to pick and choose."

Troy didn't accept that he was trying to pick and choose. He was only trying to keep her safe. Any man would do that for the woman he loved.

Vegas canted his head to the monitor. "Look at the clock. She's going to do it this time. She's going to make it through the obstacle course."

"There's no way." But Troy took in her position on the course and the time left.

Charlie whistled under his breath.

Excitement took over Troy's stomach.

"You blow it with that woman," said Vegas, "I really am going to knock you senseless."

"Better me getting hurt than her." Troy was distracted by the monitor.

Vegas came to his feet.

Troy glared at him, half expecting to get into a fight.

But Vegas took a step toward the door. "Somebody's got to be down there to meet her."

"That'll be me." Troy wasn't letting anyone else near her.

"Then you'd better offer her a job," said Vegas.

Everything inside Troy rebelled.

He couldn't. He wouldn't. Then again, how could he not?

"Your choice," said Vegas. "But if you don't, I will. There's no way Pinion is passing on a candidate with her scores."

"I'll go," Troy repeated.

"And?" Vegas prompted.

"And I'll hire her," Troy ground out.

He turned on his heel, brushing past Charlie to stomp into the hall.

How could she do it? She was about to defy the odds, to defy logic, maybe even defy the laws of physics. She was one in a million, one in a billion. She wanted what she wanted, and he was powerless to say no. He was madly, passionately, hopelessly in love with her.

Then his footsteps grew lighter as he trotted down the stairs.

He was offering her a job. And then he was offering her a ring. And then he was begging her to spend the rest of her life with him and with Drake.

He burst through the back exit, sprinting toward the finish line of the obstacle course. She was a quarter mile away, running her heart out as the seconds ticked down on the clock.

She was going to make it.

She *had* to make it.

Suddenly, her ankle gave way beneath her. She fell to the dirt, and his heart lodged in his throat. He had to forcibly stop himself from rushing to her aid.

She pulled herself to her feet. She staggered a few steps, losing precious time.

"Come on, Mila," he said under his breath.

She broke to a jog, then to a run, steadier with each step.

There was less than a minute left on the clock. He wanted desperately to give her more time.

Then she saw him.

Her steps slowed.

"No," he called out.

She stopped.

"No!" he shouted at her. "Go. Run. You can do it!"

He heard voices behind him and realized half the building had emptied to cheer her on.

A smile came over her face, and she started again, running faster. He backed off, over the line to wait for her to get there.

She closed in on it while the crowd counted down the seconds.

She made it across with six seconds left, and Troy punched a fist in the air. He grabbed her, hugging her tight around the waist, hoisting her muddy body into the air.

"You're hired," he told her. "You are so, *so* hired."

Then he kissed her while the crowd rushed around, patting her on the shoulders, congratulating her.

He slowly lowered her to the ground.

She was grinning from ear to ear.

"Charlie," he said, never taking his gaze off Mila. "Better get someone to build a new locker room."

"Yes, boss," said Charlie.

"Everybody else?"

"Yes?" they answered in unison.

"Get out of here."

There were good-natured chuckles as they all backed off.

"Mila," he whispered, brushing her muddy hair from her sweaty forehead.

"Yes, boss?" she answered.

"You'll take the job."

"Yes."

"And will you marry me?"

Her clear green eyes went wide in her muddy face.

"I love you," he said. "I love you so much."

She hesitated for a moment.

He stilled, waiting with apprehension.

"Can I do both?" she asked in a hesitant voice.

It was his turn to grin. "I'm sure hoping you will."

"I'm hired?" she confirmed.

He laughed. "You're also engaged."

"I don't know which will make my family happier." She came up on her toes to kiss him.

He couldn't seem to stop himself from pressing his luck. "Which makes you happier?"

She brushed her hand across his cheek. "That I get to love you, and be with you, and share your entire life."

"Good answer, my love. We are going to make one heck of a team."

* * * * *

If you liked this tale of instant family,
pick up these other baby stories from
New York Times *and* USA TODAY *bestselling author*
Barbara Dunlop

BILLIONAIRE BABY DILEMMA
THE MISSING HEIR

Available now from Harlequin Desire!

And don't miss the next Billionaires and Babies story
STRANDED WITH THE BOSS
from Elizabeth Lane
Available October 2015!

If you're on Twitter, tell us what you think of
Harlequin Desire! #harlequindesire.

COMING NEXT MONTH FROM

HARLEQUIN® *Desire*

Available October 6, 2015

#2401 A CONTRACT ENGAGEMENT • by Maya Banks
In this reader-favorite story, billionaire businessman Evan Ross has special terms for Celia Taylor, the sexy ad executive desperate to seal a career-making deal. But she's turning the tables with demands of her own...

#2402 STRANDED WITH THE BOSS
Billionaires and Babies • by Elizabeth Lane
Early tragedy led billionaire Dragan to steer clear of children. But could a spunky redhead—who's suing his company!—and her twin toddlers melt his frozen heart when they're stranded together in a winter cabin?

#2403 PURSUED
The Diamond Tycoons • by Tracy Wolff
Nic Durand had a one-night stand with the reporter exposing corruption in his company. Now she's having his child. She may be set on bringing him down, but he'll pursue her until he has her right where he wants her!

#2404 A ROYAL TEMPTATION
Dynasties: The Montoros • by Charlene Sands
When Princess Portia Lindstrom shows up at his coronation, it's love at first sight for King Juan Carlos. But soon her family's explosive secret could force the unwavering royal to choose between his country's future and his own.

#2405 FALLING FOR HER FAKE FIANCÉ
The Beaumont Heirs • by Sarah M. Anderson
Frances Beaumont needs a fortune. CEO Ethan Logan needs a Beaumont to give him credibility when he takes over the family brewery. Can this engagement of convenience lead to the real deal?

#2406 HIS 24-HOUR WIFE
The Hawke Brothers • by Rachel Bailey
Their spontaneous Vegas marriage should have ended the day after it began! But when they partner on a project, Adam and Callie must pretend they're still together to avoid a high-profile scandal. Will they soon want more than a short-term solution?
